The Beaufort Bride

Book One

of

The Beaufort Chronicle

Judith Arnopp

Dedication
The Beaufort Chronicles are dedicated to my mother, Doreen Lily Robson, 1923-2015.
Thank you for the love and for introducing me to books and the bard.

Other books by Judith Arnopp:
The Beaufort Woman
The King's Mother
Sisters of Arden
A Song of Sixpence: The story of Elizabeth of York and Perkin
Warbeck
Intractable Heart: The story of Kathryn Parr
The Kiss of the Concubine: A story of Anne Boleyn
The Winchester Goose: At the court of Henry VIII
The Song of Heledd
The Forest Dwellers
Peaceweaver

The Lady Margaret

It is a wild night. Outside, the trees are blackened by rain. They thrash their limbs in a dance of anguish, shedding leaves and twigs across the lawn, but here, at the nursery window, I am safe and dry. I press my hot cheek against cool thick glass and peer into the darkness of the garden.

The shrubs and hedges assume threatening shapes; the yew tree by the gatehouse is a hump of deep black menace. My seven-year-old mind forgets the times my stepsisters and I have happily played there on the green mead in the sunshine; tonight I see only threats, only danger, only demons.

A fistful of raindrops spatters against the window and I draw back with a gasp as a yellow leaf, as large as my face, smacks suddenly onto the glass. I stare at it, stuck there like a hand held up in warning. Do not look, Margaret!

But I do look. I cannot help it. If there is a beast in the garden, I have to see it. I have to witness the moment it leaps from the darkness.

Ever since I can remember the grown-ups have kept secrets from me. I didn't know my mother had been married before, that my siblings had a different father to mine. It was Oliver who told me, and ever since he has delighted in revealing other, more horrible things. Now,

1

to deny him pleasure, I am determined to learn secrets for myself. Secrets that are sometimes best left undiscovered.

No one tells me when I am made a ward of the Duke of Suffolk, fated to marry whomever he pleases. It is Oliver who breaks the news and, at first, I don't believe him.

"Don't be silly," I scowl. "Stop teasing."

"Oh, I'm not teasing."

He slides from his seat and comes skulking toward me, his head thrust forward, a grin of mischief smeared across his dirty face. "You have to do as he says and go happily to your marriage, even if he weds you to a grandfather who will beat you twice daily."

"He wouldn't do that."

I can hear the doubt in my own voice and it spurs him on to greater revelations.

"He can do with you as he wishes and you have to obey him or, if you don't, you'll be shut up in the Tower as your father would have been if he hadn't -"

A sudden movement and Edith comes to stand beside me. She places her hand on my arm.

"Oliver, be quiet. You are being cruel. Don't listen to him, Margaret, just ignore him. Why don't you come and help me sort colours for the tapestry I am planning?"

Edith, my older and favourite sister, grabs my wrist and tries to tug me toward her chair but, drawn to the awfulness of Oliver's secret, I pull away.

"What do you mean, Oliver? My father in the Tower; what do you mean?"

He stands tall, runs two fingers across his upper lip, presenting a sudden image of how he will look when he is a man with a fine moustache and beard. His head is back and he squints down his long nose with a smirk. He is no longer a companion of the nursery; he is an accuser, a torturer, a devil with wickedness upon his lips.

"Your father was a traitor, waiting to be sent to the Tower. The king was going to chop off his head ... but your father sliced his own wrists before he could be taken."

With a gasp of horror, my stepsisters look up from the hearth where they are sewing. Everyone is looking at me. My cheeks begin to burn. I can feel their eyes boring into me, waiting for my reaction. I cannot move; my ears are ringing. It is as if he has struck me but I manage to raise my chin and clench my lips across my teeth.

Oliver watches my struggle for composure, but his venom is subsiding. He is clearly calculating our mother's reaction should I run to her with the tale of his sins.

It takes a great deal of effort to shrug my shoulders and turn away as if nothing is amiss. His uncertain laughter follows my stiff-legged journey toward the door. I reach for the latch but before I pass through it, I feel Edith's hand on my shoulder.

"Margaret, don't believe him. He heard it from the servants – it is likely just tittle-tattle."

I look into her kind eyes and read the lie hidden there. She seeks to spare my hurt, but I can tell she believes the story. I try to smile but my mouth goes out of shape, my chin trembling. She places a gentle hand on my coif but I shake it off, cuff away the first tear before it has a chance to drip onto my cheek.

I find Mother just returned from chapel. She halts when she sees me and hands her prayer book to one of her women.

"Margaret? What is the matter? Are you ill?"

I shake my head and perform a wobbly curtsey.

"No Mother, I am well."

She sits down and beckons me closer, places a hand beneath my chin. She feels my brow for signs of fever, pulls down my lower eye lid and bids me stick out my tongue. I obey, passively waiting while she examines my teeth and looks in my ears.

"You are very pale, and you are trembling. What has happened? Have you been fighting again?"

"No, Mother." Although I threaten to, I never bear tales of Oliver's taunting. I search around in my head for a small lie that will explain how I have heard the rumour of my father's disgrace. "I heard someone talking."

She sits back, links her fingers and rests her hands on her stomach.

"You should never heed gossip, Margaret."

"No, I don't but ... they said bad things about my father."

I watch her face blanch and know without her confirmation that Oliver's tale is true. Her face squirms unattractively as she tries to school her features into obedience.

"Who have you been listening to?"

"Oh ... I – I don't know. We were playing hide-come-seek and I was hiding in a cupboard when some servants were passing ... I couldn't see who it was."

I will have to make confession and do penance for such a lie, but I refuse to bear tales. It will only make Oliver resent me more.

"Is it true, Mother?" I step closer. "Was my father a bad man? Did he ... did he ...?"

I cannot form the last words and as my fear spills from my eyes, her own composure dissolves. She fumbles for a kerchief, blows her nose.

"Oh, Margaret." She screws the square of linen into a ball and looks at the ceiling. "Your father was a good man, an honest man but ... well, he was not always wise. He made mistakes in France and angered the king. When King Henry refused him an audience, your father fell into despair. I ... we are not sure what happened ... it was a long time ago, six years."

I listen to the horrid truth, counting back the years on my fingers. 1443, the year I was born.

"So, if my father was a traitor, are we all disgraced? Am I a disgrace? Am I, Mother?"

She sighs, casts about for her kerchief again and dabs her nose.

"No. Your great uncle, the Cardinal, and your uncle Edmund will ensure we remain in the king's good graces. You must learn that everything is not black and white, or good and evil. There are many different shades. Your father was neither; he was just a man, and all men make mistakes ... even kings."

The end of her sentence is barely audible. I jerk my head and stare into her eyes, trying to fathom what she means. I have been taught an anointed king is sacrosanct. It has never occurred to me that kings can err.

"So the king was wrong?"

"Mistaken, perhaps, is a better word; an error of judgement."

"What about us? Is Oliv - are the servants right when they say that I must marry whomever the Duke says?"

She looks around the room, her lashes fluttering like damp butterflies that cannot decide upon which blossom to settle.

"We must all marry where we can, Margaret. A woman is seldom given choice."

"But what if he picks an old man who will beat me twice a day?"

The words are out before I can stop them, Oliver's laughter echoing again in my ears. She pauses with the kerchief just below her nose.

"No! Where do you get such ideas, child? Come here."

I long to slide onto the chair beside her and inhale her sweet herby scent that speaks of security. I wish I could snuggle to her bosom. If she was not big with child I could crawl into her lap as if I were a baby. She places her hand upon her swollen belly. "I suppose it is time I told you of your future. You are an important asset to the Duke but he has chosen very carefully for you."

"Who will want to marry me when my father was so bad?"

She laughs musically, tilting her head back. "Oh my dear child, do you not realise how rich you are? You are an heiress and will be an asset to any husband. Men have already been seeking the honour of your hand."

I digest this news slowly. So, Oliver was right. I am to be sold.

"You said 'chosen' so the Duke has already decided?"

Her hand, that has been gently rubbing the place where her unborn child is curled, stops suddenly. She smiles and looks down at it. She has felt the child kick – another half-sibling. I will no longer be the smallest. I will no longer be the baby of the family. I pray this child will be kinder than Oliver.

"The Duke fancies you for his son, John, who is destined to be a great man."

I have seen the Duke of Suffolk many times, the great William de la Pole who has fought so long for the king in France. Oliver says that he has almost single-handedly kept our territories in English hands. He is a favourite of the king, but the populace dislike him and have christened him 'Jackanapes.'

The duke is a big man, large and rough. I remember when I was little, hiding behind my mother's chair when he came into her parlour. His giant frame blocked the sun from the window and his laugh made the wine cups rattle on their tray. I am filled with dread that his son will be the same.

"Suppose I do not like him?" I whisper with sickness washing in my belly. Mother smiles and closes one eye before answering conspiratorially.

"Then you will make the best of him, as do all women in our position."

February 1450

"Margaret, it is time to wake up; the Matins bell has rung."

I roll over with a groan and blink at Edith who is leaning over me. Her long fair hair has worked its way out of her cap and is tumbling about her shoulders. "Come on, sleepyhead," she laughs. Grabbing my wrist, she hauls me from the bed.

I stand for a while, staring dull-wittedly at the floor while my body slowly wakes, my mind gathers itself. I lift my chin, remembering that this is my last day. Tomorrow I am to be married.

Fear clutches at my belly. I have always had the protection of my mother and my stepfather, John Welles, but now I am to be handed into the keeping of the Duke and his son, who is soon to be my husband.

My clothes press is stuffed with new linen, new shoes, a fine brocade gown and a fancy new *escoffion* and veil. Such care has never before been taken with my clothes and, although I normally have little interest in such things, I feel different when I try them on. The girl in the looking glass is nothing like me. I look and feel important, grown-up and noble. It is only my eyes that look like my own: large, dark and terrified.

This morning, I am so frantic to stay that I am filled with a desperate love for everything familiar. I smile at my nurse with new appreciation as she dresses me. When she kneels to slip on my shoes I put a hand on her shoulder and whisper, "Thank you." She looks up in surprise, as if I have never thought to thank her before.

"Here you are, my lady." She hands me my prayer book, and my stepsisters and I hurry toward chapel. As we clatter along the corridor, we are met by Oliver and our eldest brother, John, who are emerging from their chamber. The two boys jostle to be head of the procession until Mother appears at the door, her belly standing proud before her.

She has not long to go now; after my wedding she will retire to her chambers to await the arrival of her child. She is shadowed about the eyes and her face is puffy. She raises one eyebrow in reprimand and the boys immediately fall into submission. They play the part of great gentlemen, bowing and holding out their arms that she might go ahead. She smiles indulgently.

"Come, Margaret," she says and, with an apologetic grimace at my sisters, I push my way to the front and take my position just a little behind Mother. Although I am the youngest daughter, I am afforded the most honour because of the status of my father, who was the

Duke of Somerset. My uncle Edmund has that honour now.

I would rather sit with Edith. I cast a glance over my shoulder and she sends me a funny, upside down smile, raises a hand and waggles her fingers. As I pass my brothers I keep a wary eye on Oliver in case he puts out a foot to trip me. Silence falls as we follow Mother into the chapel, make our obeisance to the lofty cross and take our places for prayer.

The words of the psalms echo in the vaulted roof, the morning sun shines through multi-coloured glass casting patterns on the floor, red and yellow and blue. The sing-song voice of the priest enters my soul. I clasp my hands, close my eyes and pray fervently to the lord to help me accept the path He has chosen for me.

If I am to bear this marriage I must either learn to like my husband or pray to soon be made a widow. Shocked by the wicked, unbidden thought of John de la Pole's early death, I pray harder and know myself a sinner. "Let us be happy, Lord," I pray. "Please give us happiness."

I do not sleep a wink. Not for one moment does my mind let me rest. When dawn finally breaks I rise reluctantly, and after mass my chamber fills with servants. They form a chain bearing buckets of steaming water to fill the bath that is set before the hearth. Flower petals are strewn on the surface and thick towels are placed near the hearth to benefit from the flames.

When they strip me of my clothes, I cross my hands across my skinny chest and lower myself into water that is barely warm. Then, with small consideration given to my status, I am scrubbed from head to toe, my hair is washed, and my nails clipped. I stand on a towel before the fire while they rub me dry and comb the knots from my soaking hair. I shiver, my body swathed in goosebumps as they rub fragrant lotion into my skin. Soon, I quake inside my fine new clothes. Every scrap of hair is tucked inside my hood, making my eyes seem bigger than ever, my face bony and white. I am no beauty and, as I regard the stranger in the mirror, I realise that even fine fashion will never make me so.

As we process to the church, I can hear Mother's breath rasping. I look up at her and notice the beads of sweat collecting on her upper lip. She tries to smile but I can see her discomfort; the child lies heavy in her womb making her usually quick steps lumbering and slow. I spare her a moment from my own concerns and take her arm, slow my pace a little.

The priest who leads our small procession is unaware that we have slowed and reaches the porch before us. He turns, opens his mouth to speak and looks surprised to find us lagging. He clasps his wrist and, with a benign smile, waits patiently for our approach.

I wish I could turn and run but I am Lady Margaret Beaufort, about to become the wife of the Duke of Suffolk's heir. Girls like me cannot be like infants and run away. We must put aside our childhood and act like women, and make the best of what we are given.

In the porch my ladies fuss with the hem of my gown, Mother strokes a wisp of hair from my face, left loose today in testimony to my innocence. The choir begins to sing, their voices fuelling my courage and reviving my faith that God will steer my course. I take a deep breath and step into the darkness of the nave.

In the dim light, the duke is waiting. It is the first time I have seen him without a sword, and he looks ill at ease without it. He is finely garbed in thick velvet, and the hat he turns in his hand is hung with jewels. Beside him, a boy, a few years older than me and as richly clad as his father, is biting his thumb. The duke slaps the boy's hand from his mouth and I see tears spring to his eyes. I cannot stop myself from staring at him.

Why, why, why has nobody told me? I turn my head and see Oliver is grinning, his eyes filled with jovial tears. I realise he has known all along, his stories of a bullying brute have all been for my discomfort. I have been expecting a man, a fully grown tyrant in the image of his father, but here is a skinny boy, and clearly we will not be expected to live together for many years. I tug at Mother's sleeve, give a wobbly smile. She stoops so I can whisper in her ear.

"Is that him?"

She nods, strokes my hair. "Do you think you can like him?"

I shrug, a shadow of doubt returning.

"Will I have to go away with them?"

"No, no." Her denial is adamant and surprised. "Whatever gave you that idea?"

My relief is great but I glare once again at Oliver, who sobers suddenly as Mother's eye follows my gaze. The choir ceases, the priest steps forward to the altar and silence falls like a heavy blanket on a flame.

I am prodded forward, and with shaking steps I stand shoulder to shoulder with John, who is to be my husband. As he makes his vow, his voice is high-pitched, shaky, and he stops in the middle to sniff. But when it is my turn I clear my throat and answer loud and strong, so that my voice will be heard even at the back of the church.

At the wedding feast we are seated side by side but John says very little. He nibbles at his food like a mouse, leaves half-chewed morsels that are not to his liking on the side of his trencher. He answers his elders meekly, as if he has learned a handful of responses by rote and dare not stray from them. I watch him rinse his fingers in the bowl provided; his hands are thin, his nails bitten to the quick, and his wrists are bony. I can't imagine he will ever grow as big as his father.

Oliver says that the Duke is out of favour with King Henry and his French queen just now, but is a great warrior; a 'veteran of war' he calls him. I glance sideways at his son and try to picture John at sword play, if indeed he has begun to train for a soldier as Oliver has.

As the minstrel steps onto the floor, I pick up a wafer and sink my teeth into it, enjoying the rush of honey on my tongue. If I am clever and act quickly, I can prevent this little boy from bullying me as Oliver does. I might be just a girl but I sense his weakness, his uncertainty. I must be shrewd, hide my shyness and take control to ensure he never becomes my master.

<u>April 1450</u>

I find that although I am now a wife, nothing has changed. I remain at home with Mother, where Oliver continues to tease me in the nursery, and my lessons go on as before. John is to be raised elsewhere. He must learn the skills of the battlefield, and how to be the master of his own house. I see little of him, but he is brought for a visit in early April.

Spring comes late this year and we have to wrap up warmly against the breeze whenever we go outside. John, when he comes, pays little attention to me. Instead, he tumbles in the meadow with Oliver, and I begin to worry that he will learn my brother's bullying habits.

My sisters and I are searching for bird nests in the gardens when Oliver and John come running back from the meadow. They are dirty; Oliver has torn his hose and John has lost his cap. They slump on the damp grass at our feet, their faces rosy from their downhill race. For the duration of John's visit Oliver has been excused his studies, but my morning has been spent at lessons and prayer. I suffer a pang of resentment at their freedom. It must be so much better to be a boy. I don't believe my face has ever been allowed to get as dirty as theirs are, and I am certain Edith's hasn't.

"Do you know what is happening, Oliver?" Edith asks. "There have been messengers coming and going all morning."

Oliver plucks an emerging dandelion and begins to tear the bud apart.

"I expect it is about the latest fighting in France."

Our world is governed by war, battle-hardened warriors holding on to the crown for our wavering king. The women stay indoors to pray. I am told time and time again that a woman's place is at home. I wonder what it would be like to be a man and ride out at the head of an army. I know of only one woman who attempted that, and we all know how Joan, the maid of Orleans, ended up. It is safer to stay at home.

I cross myself rapidly and send up a silent prayer for her poor soul before turning my attention back to my brother, who is giving us the details of the battle.

"The king must be furious at such a loss. It is a major blow for England. We can't afford to lose any more territory."

He glances at John, who flushes red. Even I recognise the unspoken accusation. Rumour and gossip of the Duke's unpopularity finds a way even into our nursery, and we are all aware of the problems he is having.

"My father isn't to blame." John says, closing one eye and squinting up at the sulky sun. "He advises the king but he doesn't listen. He and Queen Margaret make the mistakes and my father takes the blame. The people hate him when it is the king they should berate."

"I am sure everything will work out." Edith leans forward, places her fingers on John's sleeve. He gives a half smile, shrugs his shoulders as if he doesn't care either way, but I know he does.

I furrow my brow, struggling to understand. The duke is an important man, I know that much. Oliver is always telling me he is the chamberlain of England, captain of Calais, warden of the Cinque Ports and other such honours. Of course, I am not sure what these titles are, or what they mean, but as long as the duke is powerful and John is safe, so will I be. But if he loses the friendship of the king, what will happen to us? My father was driven to suicide by the withdrawal of the king's love, and it is something I cannot forget.

"The king is weak." Oliver rolls onto his back and stares at the sky, where early swallows are soaring. "He should tell his wife to be quiet. She should keep her nose out of politics and concentrate on getting him an heir."

Oliver is quoting our stepfather, John Welles, whom I have often heard say such things. He loves the king but wishes he were wiser and stronger. Edith sighs; she is sitting so close to me that I feel her ribs heave.

"The poor lady; she must be so sad not to have a son yet."

"What will happen if she doesn't? Who will be king when King Henry dies?"

I drop my voice to a whisper and we exchange glances. While my brother knots his brow, trying to recall his lessons, I lean forward, tucking my hands beneath my armpits, waiting for an answer. Oliver sits up, crosses his legs, his grass-stained knee poking through the rip in his hose. He wrinkles his nose.

"I think the Duke of York is next in line – his mother was a Mortimer. Of course, if the Beauforts weren't excluded from the succession, you could be queen, Margaret."

At first, I don't grasp his meaning. I stare at his grinning face for several moments before the words sink in. John is suddenly alert. He slaps his own knee.

"That would be good. Margaret could be queen and I'd be the King of England."

He raises his chin and assumes what he thinks is a lordly air. He looks like a buffoon. They are all laughing. Oliver punches John's upper arm and they begin rolling on the grass. My sisters look on smiling, but I am very, very still.

"What rubbish you talk, Oliver," I call loudly over their ruckus. "I'd not be queen for all the riches in the world."

The boys sober. Oliver and John begin to search the grass for beetles, while Edith, Mary and Eliza discuss new gowns for Easter. I take no part in their chatter but sit quietly, imaging a world where girls are allowed to ascend the throne of England and wear a golden crown.

"The Duke of Suffolk is under arrest in the Tower!" Oliver dashes into the room, making me start, the needle jabbing into my finger. While my sisters leap to their feet, I watch a bead of emerging blood smear across the row of puckered stitches. I poke my finger into my mouth; a metallic rasp burning upon my tongue as I raise my eyes to Oliver's.

For once, he is not teasing. He pushes through our clamouring sisters and comes to sit softly beside me at the window. He smells of the outdoors; grass and wind and rain. My heart hammers beneath my ribs.

"What will happen? What about John?" I whisper. "He will be so afraid. I shall write to him."

"You had better ask Mother for permission before you do. She might wish you to wait to see what happens."

I have often imagined how it might have been for my father falling foul of the king, and it is easy to imagine John's fear. He is not a brave boy like Oliver, although he tries very hard to be.

"The king will forgive him, won't he? You said the duke was his friend."

Oliver almost undoes his kindness by giving a short bitter snort of derision. Then he remembers himself and smiles at me as if I am his dearest sister. His voice is soft as he carefully explains.

"Kings can't afford to be friends with the wrong people. My tutor says York and his followers have made Suffolk a scapegoat for the king's misgovernment. If the king shows him too much support, he may find himself in the firing line."

"The king? That can't happen, surely." Edith, who has come to sit at my other side, squeezes my hand. "I am sure it will all blow over and things will go back to normal. Shall we go to Mother and ask if we can send a message to John?"

She holds out her hand and, with a smile of thanks to Oliver, I slide from the seat and go with her to our mother's apartment.

"No, do not write," Mother says. "Not until we can learn more. Perhaps by tomorrow the duke will have been released." She is pacing the floor, her face white with strain. The birth of my baby brother last month went hard with her, and she has only recently left the lying-in chamber. "I will write to your stepfather for advice, but for now we must do nothing. We do not want to draw attention to ourselves."

The next few days are void of news, but Oliver speculates endlessly. We grow quite tired of him. One moment he swears there will be a war, the next he thinks the duke will be pardoned, and then he reverts to his certainty that disaster is close. With no word from John, we can only wonder how he is coping with the horrible uncertainty. Yet when news eventually comes, and I am summoned to Mother's apartments, I wish I was still ignorant.

"The duke is dead," Mother tells me and will say no more, but the crumpled kerchief in her fist and her tight white lips tell me quite plainly that there is more to know. I am determined to discover the truth.

"It will be all right, Mother," I venture, bravely placing my hand on her knee. "Perhaps John can live with us now, here at Bletsoe."

She stands up, and my hand falls away. "Don't be ridiculous, Margaret. Go back to the nursery. Send Edith to me, there is a matter I wish to discuss with her."

So many questions burn within my mind, but the stiff straight back that is turned toward me prevents me from speaking. I hesitate for a long moment, switching my weight from one foot to the other until she becomes impatient. She spins around, her brows an angry furrow.

"I said I wish to speak to Edith."

I sketch a brief curtsey before fleeing her presence, and hurry to rejoin the others in the nursery. They all look up when I enter the room.

"What did she say?" Oliver puts down his book, his face anxious.

"Nothing. Just that the duke is dead. She would say nothing more, nothing about how he died or what John will do now. Oh, and she wants to speak to Edith."

Edith stands up with a sigh, pausing at the door as John speaks.

"I think your marriage might be annulled."

I look up quickly. "Ended, you mean. I won't be his wife after all?"

The idea is startling. I had thought my future settled, and suddenly a black wall of uncertainty rears before me. I can see Oliver thinking, searching for a way to explain the intricacies of the world to me, a girl who knows nothing of how it all works.

"Mother and Father will see no benefit to a union with the son of a traitor. John will lose his inheritance and so our parents will seek to find favour with the king, and secure a marriage contract that will bring you the prestige you deserve."

Edith quietly closes the door.

"Oh," I whisper, wishing she would come back.

I find I have grown used to the idea of John; a boy young enough to be my friend, a boy who will not order me around. The old uncertain fears stir again.

18

In bed that night, while the others gossip I pretend to sleep. I burrow beneath the blankets, making sure one ear remains above the pillows. I keep my breathing deep and regular while the whispering voices of my sisters hiss in the dark.

"Oliver told me what really happened, but if I tell you, you are not to breathe a word to Margaret. She is too young to know such things."

I hold my breath. The bed ropes groan beneath us as Eliza and Agnes wriggle closer to Edith.

"We won't say a word, I swear," Eliza whispers. Edith takes a deep breath.

"Oliver says the king loved the duke and wanted to forgive him, but the commons wouldn't let him. In the end, the king caved in beneath their pressure and sentenced him, not to death, but to exile…"

Beneath the covers, I frown to myself. Surely, this news is good; exile is harsh but it can't be as bad as death. Edith's voice continues.

"He left the Tower in great secrecy but was accosted by a mob at his house at St Giles and had to escape like a felon out the back door. Last week he managed to take to sea, but before he had left English waters his vessel was intercepted by his enemies."

I know I am about to learn something terrible. My heart is beating slow and hard, so loud I am sure they will hear it. My throat closes. I need to swallow, to clear the obstruction so that I may breathe freely, but I can't. Edith pauses … I grow frantic, stifled of air, longing to throw off the covers, sit up and yell at her not to tarry with the telling of her tale. But if I do, she will stop, or alter her words to suit my tender ears. I have to know the truth, no matter how bad it is.

"What did they do to him?"

I bless Agnes for her impatience.

Edith draws a breath. I can feel her steel herself. The blankets shift as she leans even closer to our sisters, allowing a tiny trickle of air to flow across my face.

"They showed no mercy. They took him on board their ship and despite his desperate pleas for mercy, they named him a traitor. Without recourse to the law, they chopped off his head. He died unshriven, and Oliver says they left his head and body on Dover beach for the gulls to pick."

Sickness floods into my throat. I can bear it no longer. With a cry, I fight my way from the stifling blankets, sit up and struggle to the side of the bed. I hold my belly and stagger to the centre of the room. The floor seems to sway, tipping me forward to vomit on the smooth polished wood. Drool and tears and snot dribble down my chin, my cheeks are wet, and my heart is hammering.

"Margaret!" Edith's face is slack with horror. She climbs from the mattress and rushes forward to help me back to bed on trembling limbs. I flop upon the pillow, draw the back of my hand across my lips and look at my sisters, who are staring open-mouthed.

"Oh, Margaret, I thought you were sound asleep."

I stare at Edith, still unable to speak, my mind teeming with images of John's father's untimely death. She sits down beside me and my head droops on her shoulder, her fingers soft in my hair. "You won't tell Mother, will you, Margaret? I will be in such trouble if you do."

After that, my dreams are haunted. Each night I wake up panting in the darkness. I shake my head trying to dislodge the bloody images from my mind. I burrow deep beneath the covers, listen to the snores of my sisters and stare sightlessly into the dark. For the first time I realise my own mortality, and that of my family. Desperately, I pray to the saints for peace of mind, beseeching God to look kindly upon me, his most humble, most obedient servant.

Slowly, as dawn creeps into the east, I can discern the outline of the window, a crack of light between the shutters. Soon, the servants are abroad, moving stealthily about the room to coax the fires back to flame. There comes a clattering from the kitchen and then the matins bell rings. I rise heavy-eyed, yawning as my woman helps me dress, and soon, the familiar routines of the morning chase away the terror of the night.

Nobody seems to notice my pink-rimmed eyes or listlessness. Mother and my stepfather are distracted by news from London of riots, fighting and insurrection. My uncle Somerset, who is great friends with the queen, is in trouble in France. Oliver says he surrendered our territory without a fight, and now the people are turning against him even more. I overhear the grown-ups talking after supper; they speak of unrest, the country dividing further. The Duke of York, the king's heir, resentful at being packed off to Ireland while my uncle receives the honour he thinks should be his, is marching on London with an army of three thousand men. It seems to me that the whole world has caught the madness of the king.

While messengers scurry to and fro, and my stepfather prepares to ride to the king's aid, nobody notices my fears. I begin to think they do not care. Desperate to know all there is to know, I linger in corners, listening, watching, my fear deepening as my understanding increases. In the end, I creep to the chapel and kneel alone at the altar. I interlace my fingers, press them against my chin, close my eyes and pray to God to make the nightmares cease.

But God is busy with matters of state. He spares no time for me. I am just a little girl.

The ship is foundering. Great waves wash across the rain-lashed deck where I cling for life to a slither of slimy green rope. I blink through darkness, open my mouth and scream for my mother, but she is not here. She is bending over my infant brother's cot, crooning a nursery tune that she used to sing to me. All I have is a slippery rope and my grip is loosening.

Someone grabs me by the collar and drags me to the centre of the deck. A huge figure, horned and red, towers above me. He looks like the devil, his breath as foul as my uncle's hunting dogs, his eyes a fiery red. His hand is hard on my neck, and in his other fist he clutches a rusty axe.

He pushes me down, down, his hand on my throat so I cannot breathe. I fight against him but I am too small, too weak. I open my eyes to a great flash of lightning that strikes his blade, turning it as red as the coals in the blacksmith's forge. I want to scream but I have no breath; my kicks and struggles are nothing to him. "Please God," I gasp. "Free me from my enemies. Keep me safe, guide my path."

The muscles on the beast's naked torso ripple, the axe is falling in a great arc. My eyes are transfixed by its journey, which seems to take forever ... all my life I have been here, waiting for ignominious death ...

"Margaret, wake up! You are dreaming! Margaret, wake up!"

"Edith!" I fall sobbing into her arms and feel her hands soft on my hair.

"Hush," she croons. "It is all right, you are awake now. It was just a dream."

I cannot tell her of my nightmare for a long time. Not until my chest ceases to shudder and my throat is no longer clenched so tight. When I try to explain, although I cannot put the full horror of it into words, she opens her eyes wide.

"Poor Margaret, how awful," she says.

"What are dreams, Edith? Why do we have them?"

"I am not sure. My old nurse used to say they were a message from beyond the grave but ... I am not sure."

She half smiles, then frowns, her eyes serious. "I expect you are just over-tired, or perhaps you ate something at supper that disagreed with you."

She smiles, satisfied to have discovered a reason. But each time I close my eyes I can still see the devil's face, feel his fist clamped tight on my throat. He is real, I know it; he is real and waiting to claim us should we stray from God's path. I am sure the dream was summoned by something more than a piece of meat that should have been thrown to the dogs. I begin to think of all the people I know who are dead; my father, and the duke ... I shake myself and briskly rub my arms in a futile attempt to chase off the lingering horror.

I decide to pray more often. Even if my knees become raw from kneeling on the stone floor, I will pray as much and for as long as I can. Only God can keep the devil at bay; perhaps that is the message behind the dream. Perhaps I have inadvertently sinned and the only way to make penance is to constantly pray.

I pray, not just for myself, but also for the king to wake up from the illness that has seized him, making him as ineffectual as a babe in arms. I pray for the queen, whose attempt to govern during her husband's sickness earns her more enemies by the day. I also pray for John de la Pole, whom I am no longer encouraged to love. I wonder what will become of him now. I wish I could write to him, tell him of my sadness at his plight, but I am forbidden. It seems that during a lucid moment, the king and my stepfather have agreed that our marriage is no longer desirable.

Until it happened, I had no idea that marriages were so easily made and broken. When our hands were joined two years ago, I imagined only God could break the union. I was wrong.

February 1453

I am to accompany my mother to court to be presented to the king and queen. Trying to conceal their envy, my sisters look on as I am fitted once more for new clothes. The brocade is stiff and uncomfortable. It scratches beneath my chin, and when they dress my hair it is pulled so tight beneath my hennin that it makes my scalp smart. And the new shoes are pinching – usually I hate new shoes, but looking down at the red leather toes peeking from beneath my gown, I have to concede they are very fine.

"Now, you must remember to be meek yet pleasant, proud yet kind; do you understand?"

I frown as Mother leans forward and plucks a stray hair from my brow, making my eyes water. She adjusts her girdle, lifts her chin and winks at me.

"Stay close, walk slowly, keep a smile on your face, but direct it at none but the king and queen. Address nobody unless I do first, and then be careful what you say."

My heart throbs as I follow her from the chamber and pass along the corridor. A serving girl ducks into an alcove to allow us to pass, her head lowered. She bobs a curtsey when I draw near but I have been told that servants are beneath my notice, so I keep my gaze averted. Mother dips her high headdress beneath a low lintel and we negotiate the stairs. Below, as we approach the assembly, the din increases; a babble of voices merging to form nonsense.

A clarion of trumpets shatters the conversation and silence falls; my heart quails further as all eyes turn upon us. An authoritative voice calls out our names: "Lady Margaret Welles and Lady Margaret Beaufort."

Mother moves regally forward and I follow, doing my best to glide as I have been taught. In my mind, I can hear the voice of my old nurse, "You are not a goose, Lady Margaret, so do not walk like one." As we pass into the room, the court turns toward us with a loud shuffling of feet and marks our progress toward the dais. Every person in the room, great and small, is judging us, speculating.

I try to remember Mother's instruction. I paste a smile on my face, keep my eyes on the back of her neck, my chin lifted, my neck stretched. As we move closer to the king and queen, the colours of the courtiers clothes either side of us blur into a pattern of vibrant hues. Mother halts and sinks to her knees, and after a moment's hesitation, I do the same, my skirts forming a vibrant pool around me.

"Get up, get up ..." The king has risen from his throne and hurries forward, fussing like an old mother hen. He takes my mother's arm to help her rise and pats her awkwardly. "My very dear cousin, we are happy to have you here ... delighted, delighted."

He smiles agreeably, hesitates and glances at me, opening his hands in joy and bringing them down on his knees, stooping so we are of a height. "Can this be little Margaret?" he asks, his nose an inch from mine.

Unsure what to do but remembering Mother's instruction not to speak before she does, I sink to my knees again. I dislike being called 'Little Margaret,' but it is an appellation often applied to me. I am small, much smaller than my siblings, and Mother says I have bones like a bird.

Lifting her head so that all present may hear her words, Mother speaks at last.

"We are happy to be here, Your Grace."

In rising to greet us, the king has not adhered to etiquette and Mother does her best to disguise the fact. She opens her arm and brings me forward so I may be presented to the queen. Anxiously, I lay my eyes on King Henry's consort.

Margaret of Anjou waits for our approach. Her eyes sweep across my frame, taking in my fine clothes, my sweating brow, before returning her gaze to Mother.

"Lady Welles and Lady Margaret, you are welcome to our court."

She is not what I had expected. Her voice is heavily accented yet soft, and her eyes are kind. I stand stiffly, not knowing what to say as Mother and the queen discuss the weather, and the newly refurbished hall.

The king hovers nearby. He clasps his hands as if he would rather be praying; his shoulders are a little hunched, his gaze not settling on any one thing or person. While we wait for him to speak, my uncle, the Duke of Somerset, steps forward and ushers him back to his seat. The king follows obediently like a small boy, and I remember Oliver's tales of his instability. I had never quite believed his stories of the mad king ruled by his queen and her chief advisor, Somerset. Now, I can see there may be some truth in them. I wrack my brains, trying to remember all Oliver has told me of the goings on at court.

There is a long-standing resentment between Somerset and the king's heir, the Duke of York. Some say King Henry wishes to make Somerset his heir in York's stead. Slowly and deservedly, York is being ousted, and Somerset receives all the favour, and all the while the king remains deaf to York's demands for more say in the government of the country. As I recall, after the riots of recent years, the duke has now quit the court, refusing even the summons from the king.

Oliver has told me of the ill will directed at the queen whose unpopularity with the common people increases with every passing day. The realm is quiet again now, but Oliver still believes my uncle Somerset to be at the helm of a foundering ship.

I remember my dream again, the great thundering storm, the devil's grip on my throat – I shudder. Mother, ever vigilant, turns to me.

"Are you chilly, Margaret?"

"Oh no, I am quite warm, thank you, Mother."

"She has not an ounce of flesh on her bones, no wonder she is chilled." The queen smiles, her stretched mouth belying her white face and reddened eyes.

She has recently lost her mother, Isabella of Lorraine, and my heart twists in sympathy. I cannot imagine losing my own mother; she might be stern and sometimes a little frightening, but still she is my place of safety, my anchor. I never want to leave her. There is no one else I can trust. I would like to tell the queen of my pity, offer condolence for her sorry loss, but I remain mute, remembering I have been warned to speak only when spoken to.

She beckons to a page to bring stools and Mother and I sit at her feet. I listen as the women discuss the latest fashion, the new music.

"When the weather changes," the queen is saying, "we will visit you at Bletsoe; in the summer, when the roads are better."

Mother smiles her delight but I can see her mentally calculating the cost of a royal visit, the price of refurbishing the main chambers. Bletsoe may be grand and our coffers deep, but Mother is careful with money and always makes a point of the virtue of thriftiness.

A page pours wine and my mother sips it, savouring the taste before complimenting the queen. Slowly, as the court realises there is no gossip to be had from our meeting, they turn away and begin to chat among themselves.

Aware of a thousand eyes lingering upon me, I sit as gracefully as I can on the low stool. I clutch my fingers tightly and keep my chin so high that my neck begins to ache. Without moving my head, I look about the hall, recognising a few faces, and speculating on who the others may be.

I see two sets of courtiers, both as proud and richly clad as the other, yet somehow distinct. I try to puzzle the difference, but it escapes me. There seems to be a division. Their clothes are similar, their manners are equally as courtly, their chatter just as loud. It takes me some time to realise that one set are cheerful and ebullient, while the other group, who stand a little farther from the dais, are just the opposite. I sense discomfort and resentment.

It is not the gay romantic royal court I have read about in story books. This is no Camelot, and Henry is no Arthur. My eyes slide toward the queen; she is fair enough to be Guinevere, but she is restless, constantly fidgeting. One moment her foot is tapping, the next her fingers are drumming on the arm of her throne, and her eyes never rest in any place for very long. It is as if she is constantly searching for something, or someone.

Afterwards, in our chambers, my maid helps me from my gown. She draws off my hennin and lets my hair loose. As soon as it falls about my shoulders in a brown cloud, I massage my scalp and it prickles with relief. I lie on the bed and have just closed my eyes when Mother comes and tells me she has been summoned by the king for a private audience.

"Do not leave the chambers until I come back. Go to sleep; get some rest before the evening entertainments begin."

I lie down and close my eyes again, but my mind is teeming with images, my ears still replete with clamouring voices. The discontented queen and her kind simple husband are as different as can be from what I had imagined. My mind runs through the conversation, as I try to make sense of the small snippets of a confusing grown-up world. Eventually, my eyes grow heavy and I fall asleep; it seems just a few moments later that something wakes me. I wriggle upright and knuckle sleep from my eyes, blink at the figure sitting on my bed.

"Mother?"

"You were dead to the world," she laughs. She places a hand on my bare arm, her fingers cool. As I come fully awake, I realise how unusual it is for her to come to my chamber and sit with me like this. Usually, if she requires my presence, I am summoned to hers.

"Is anything wrong?"

"No, not wrong, but I do have some news."

"News from the king?"

"Yes." She is thoughtful for a moment, then she lifts her chin, gives half a smile as if she is not sure if she is pleased or not.

"You understand you are a person of importance, don't you? As cousins to the king, there are certain expectations placed upon us – obedience being one of them."

I nod but my heart swells with fear. I know without being told that I am about to be given some troubling, possibly unwelcome, news.

"King Henry has two half-brothers, Edmund and Jasper, and has lately called them to court, making great favourites of them. He calls them his 'uterine' brothers since they shared the same mother: Catherine of Valois."

I nod vigorously. I know all about her. Oliver took great delight in describing the scandal of the widow of Henry V who took up with the Keeper of her Wardrobe and bore him two sons in secret. Some say they made a clandestine marriage, but others, Oliver included, prefer to believe the union was immoral as well as illegal. I recall the way he relished the tale, as if it afforded him some great pleasure, but it was a scandal to me that a queen should ever demean herself so. Now, in my chamber, I am struggling to understand what this has to do with me. I give Mother an enquiring look, my brow furrowed, my heart sinking even before she speaks, before I know what she is about to say. She takes a deep breath, her words coming out in a rush as if she has to force them from her tongue.

"The king has lately made them Earls. The elder, Edmund, is the Earl of Richmond, and his brother Jasper is to be given the title of Pembroke. They are powerful and influential men indeed, and are set to rise even higher. It has been decided that you should become their ward."

I open my eyes wide and try to speak but she interrupts.

"Furthermore, it is the king's wish that when you are of an age, you and Edmund should be married. But that won't be for a year or two yet."

She adds the last few words hastily, applying them like a bandage to staunch a wound before the knife penetrates my gut and the blood begins to flow. I swallow something foreign in my throat and grope for words.

A year or two. I will be almost thirteen by then and quite grown-up; perhaps by then I will have come to understand and accept it.

"Is he nice? Is he a boy ... like John?" I conceal my hands beneath the blankets and cross my fingers, silently praying.

Please don't let him be an old man; not an old man, Lord. I couldn't bear it.

"I have not yet had the pleasure of an introduction, but I am informed that both men are pleasant. Edmund is in his early twenties, a mature man but young enough for you, I feel. It will give him time to mould you into his perfect wife."

I am not sure I want to be moulded but I say nothing. She assures me that twenty is not old, but to me it seems a great age. The contentment I had enjoyed a short time ago dwindles away. I now do not care that I have a coffer full of fine clothes and jewels; my new red shoes are no longer a source of pleasure. My destiny is to

31

be placed once more in the hands of strangers – and this time they are brothers to the king.

My future looks bleak – shackled to an old man, to be ordered around at his whim; it seems so dreadful to me that I cannot force my features into a smile. There is nothing I can do to stop the tears as they prickle at the back of my eyes. I blink rapidly in an attempt to stem them and Mother lets her hands fall into her lap in exasperation.

"The point is, Margaret, the king has no heir and it looks unlikely he will get one now. Edmund is the king's favourite; in the absence of a son, the king could very well name him heir. Should you bear a son, he could well one day be king."

I pause, my tears staunched. I look up at my mother.

"King? My son could be Henry's heir?"

She smiles, winks her right eye.

"Indeed, it is a possibility, and an idea that is certainly more appealing than having York take up the reins of England."

I relax back onto my pillow again, place my hands across my concave belly. I picture a boy, slight and dark with eyes like mine. He is sitting on a golden throne and the Archbishop is lowering a great bejewelled crown on to his head. I am at his right hand, full of pride, with tears of joy anointing my cheek. I take a deep satisfied breath and decide that perhaps the future is not looking quite so bleak after all.

My joy in the future doesn't last. Within weeks of my betrothal, my mother informs me that the queen is at last with child. My foolish dreams shatter into pieces and when she sees my stricken face, she shakes her head.

"No, Margaret. We must be seen to greet the news with great joy. The whole kingdom is rejoicing and we must let the world see that we do the same."

"Am I still to wed the Earl of Richmond?"

It is not a prospect that overjoys me. Our brief meeting showed me a handsome yet distant, distracted man. His beard was rough on the back of my hand, his cursory glance dismissive, as if my opinion of him on our first meeting was immaterial. Jasper, the younger brother, was kinder; he seemed more pliant, more conscious of my tender years and finer feelings. Edmund looks to be an uncompromising man who would rule his wife with a rod of iron. I begin to hold tentative hope that I may soon be released from this second union as I was from my first.

"The king has no plans to alter the arrangement."

Mother's words quash my hopes, although Oliver assures me the king is once again touched with madness. It seems he has fallen into some kind of state where he is oblivious to all that goes on around him. I wonder who is really behind the arrangement for my marriage.

A frown settles on my brow and remains there for days. I am to be married to a man I cannot like, a man I cannot influence, yet I am to be denied the joy of seeing my son upon the throne of England. Marriage to Edmund has no compensations now.

In the nursery at Bletsoe, in the hours between supper and bed, my brothers abandon their game of chess to indulge in their favourite pastime of court intrigue.

"Of course, everyone knows the child is not of the king's getting."

"Hush, Oliver, you will be shut up in the Tower if you are not careful."

Edith's cheeks flush at the scandal of his suggestion as she bends her head back over her needlework. Unlike Edith, I am not shocked, I am curious.

"Whose child is it then, if not the king's?"

Oliver leans forward, glances at the door and back again with pleasure in his dancing dark eyes.

"Our uncle, the Duke of Somerset, of course. Everyone knows they are lovers"

"Don't be silly!" I am aghast at first, but as the news sinks in, my shock turns to indignation. I am hungry for more; I have to know. Without wishing to seem too interested, I listen almost feverishly as he continues his dirty tale of the queen's infidelity.

As Oliver speaks, my resentment grows. I may not yet be wedded and bedded by Richmond, but I am filled with indignation that my as yet unconceived son is to be denied his right by a bastard.

Later that night when I ask for God's blessing, I add a prayer to St Nicholas asking that the queen be brought to bed of a daughter so that my own son might still one day inherit.

Mother and I return home, where she wastes no time in training me in the duties of a Countess. My sisters share the lessons, but I am the only one nagged and forced to repeat things until I have them perfectly. I must learn the latest dances, practicing until I can dance them in my sleep. Mother drags me in her wake, impressing on me the important details of running a large household. By the time of my marriage, I will be schooled in all I will ever need to know.

To me, it all seems pointless. Since the queen gave birth to a prince October last, my marriage is less desirable than ever. Yet I am nothing if not obedient, and I make no complaint as I absorb my lessons.

Today my measurements are being taken, every contour carefully noted. A little man in dusty fustian bids me hold out my arm, he squints at his tape and makes some notes upon the page. Then he writes down the measurement of my waist, the length of my leg, the span of my undeveloped chest. I stand impassively and stare from the open window, although I can see only sky.

When they are done, I join my siblings in the garden. They are almost grown now and fine marriages are arranged for them, though none so grand as mine. The king has not enough brothers to go around.

The girls are picking daisies, forming them into chains and draping them over one another's ears. They look up when they hear my footstep on the gravel path.

"Margaret, there you are. I thought Mother would never let you out. What have you been doing?"

"She was having me measured for my wedding clothes."

Somehow, saying the words makes it all the more real. My wedding is not long away. Edith drapes a chain of daisies over my head and immediately begins making another. It is something we have always done. Every June since I can remember, as if we didn't have enough real gems in our coffers, we have gathered here on the mead to fashion jewels from flora.

The sun is past its zenith, the chill beginning to creep in from the edges of the garden. Soon the house will have us in its shadow, and it will be time to wash and change for supper. The chatter of my sisters washes over me and I am suddenly sad, sad that I will have to leave here soon and no longer be part of it. We may only be half-siblings but our ties are strong; too strong, I hope, to ever be broken.

I look up at the sound of horsemen in the bailey. Oliver gives a loud halloo to alert us to their return. The dogs raise their heads from slumber and set off barking in greeting, their great tails waving like banners.

"Get down," I hear Oliver cry, "don't put your dirty great feet all over my hose."

The boys enter the garden, bringing with them a sense of the masculine freedom they enjoy. They are almost men now, soft down on their chins and their voices deepening. My brother John is laughing at Oliver's dismay at his soiled clothes. Our youngest brother, Little John, whom we have been minding, spies his beloved brothers and runs forward to swing on Oliver's arm. Oliver hoists him onto his shoulders and they slowly cross the garden to settle on the grass beside us.

"The queen of the daisies," he says in admiration of my headwear, "and her pretty maids in waiting."

"And the king's homecoming." Edith drops a ring of flowers on his head but he flushes scarlet, snatches it off and gives it to little Johnny, who plants it on the dog's head.

"What news from court?" Edith asks. She is hoping for news from her sweetheart, but Oliver snatches the opportunity for fresh gossip.

Recently, the king slipped from sanity again and left the country in turmoil. The queen, determined to keep control, demanded of the council that she be named regent, but they voted against her. Even Edmund and Jasper opposed her, and instead, the Duke of York was made Protector. To our fury, York, giving vent to his long-term hatred of our uncle, had him placed under arrest and imprisoned in the Tower.

Oliver shakes his head. "Nothing is changed," he says. "My man at court tells me the royal palace is simmering with resentment, the little prince suckles hatred at his mother's teat, and York runs roughshod over everyone. It is a sorry situation."

I run my fingers through the grass and spy some ants on the sod beneath. They run from me, intent on their own affairs, and for a moment I am drawn into another world. If I were to press my finger tip upon them I could destroy them in a moment, erase the matters that they so intently pursue. Like a great impartial god, I could obliterate their lives, their world. My finger hovers, the ants flee, but with a touch of pity, I brush my palm across the tips of the lawn and send them only an earth tremor instead of devastation. Then I sigh, roll onto my back and look at the sky as Oliver's voice continues to damn the events unfolding in London. If only the God above me would prove as compassionate to my world, and show such mercy as I bestowed upon the ants.

<u>Bletsoe - November 1455</u>

Edmund Tudor and I are married at home, in Bletsoe. I am nervous, my knees quaking beneath my stiff new gown, and he is anxious, distracted, his mind clearly on other, more important matters. A sidewise glance has shown me a handsome bridegroom in fine wedding clothes, but I dare not let my eyes linger. I stand stiffly, obediently following unspoken orders from my mother. I step forward when I am bid, kneel to pray when it is requested of me. Yet, when it is time for me to make my vow to love and honour him for as long as life allows, I discover my voice has fled. I hesitate, clear my throat and make my promise, my voice discordant, sounding thin and infantile in the vastness of the chapel.

Edmund shuffles impatiently, flicks back his long hair from his shoulder and gruffly pledges his oath. Our hands are joined by the priest, God's blessing is called down upon us, and I am a wife, a countess, and a child no longer.

The bells ring out; a counterfeit of joy in what has become a worrisome world for all of us. It has been a cheerless year. Our family is fragmenting; two of my sisters have married, and my brothers have taken their places at court. In May, when the friction between York and the queen descended into violence, my uncle of Somerset was killed at a battle in St Albans. My family plunged into mourning, looking for someone on whom to place the blame. I blame them all.

The gossips warn St Albans will prove to be the first of many skirmishes, and they may be right, for the king is in the custody - or as the duke calls it, the 'protectorship' of York, and the queen is practically under house arrest.

Edmund and his brother Jasper, seeing no gain in siding with the queen, ostensibly support York, but their primary concern is for their brother. Demented or not, he is our anointed king. It is he and the security of his realm they will serve, for as long as they may. Amid all this, we celebrate our wedding, or at least, we give the appearance of celebrating it.

We emerge from church into a chilly afternoon Edmund bows over my wrist and turns on his heel, walks determinedly toward his brother. They fall straight into conversation. For a moment, although I am a bride on her wedding day and all eyes should be upon me, I am left alone.

I stand in the gusty churchyard and watch the congregation as if I am not part of it. Cousins kiss, aunts coo over newborn nephews. They are all there. My mother, my sisters, even my nurse have gathered to see me wed. I notice Edith, who is as yet unmarried, blushing at some compliment from a neighbour. She holds fast to her skirts and puts a hand to her wimple to save it from a sudden breeze that threatens to steal it. She laughs, making her suitor smile at her beauty. Edith is lucky. He is young and comely. With no great fortune to hamper her, she may be permitted to marry where she will. My heart twists suddenly and my breath catches in my throat.

I will miss her, I will miss them all. My spirits are as heavy as stone as my throat closes in an attempt to stem childish tears. Tomorrow, I must ride away with the stranger who is now my husband and take up residence in an unfamiliar castle, in an alien land. I want to pick up my skirts and run back to my chamber, take refuge in the nursery and enjoy raspberry jelly for my supper.

Edmund is being sent to Wales to keep the king's peace. I overheard him tell my mother that it was York's doing. He is exiling the king's brothers from court to diminish their influence, get them out of the way. And I can't think of a worse place to be sent.

Oliver has told me all about Wales. The least of my fears are the sprites and evil things that dwell deep in the wet Welsh woods. The country is known for its lawlessness; ever since Owain Glyndwr rebelled against the crown there have been violent quarrels between neighbours, skirmishes and in-fighting, and now the ungovernable Gruffydd ap Nicholas is making further trouble for the crown.

"We will vanquish him in a month," my husband comments at our wedding banquet. He picks a morsel of beef from his teeth and wipes it on the white tablecloth. "Royal authority will be reinstated in no time. I will see to that."

Jasper leans forward and slices his knife through a chunk of blue veined cheese.

"I have every faith in you, Brother," he grins as he plops back into his seat. He catches my eye, winks at me. "But this is no kind of wedding talk, Ed. Your bride is falling asleep."

Falling asleep at supper is something infants do. I give myself a shake and sit taller in my seat, look across the hall, pretending interest in a trio of minstrels who are preparing for a song. Beside me, Edmund grunts noncommittally and picks up his wine cup. I hear the gulp as he dispatches the fluid down his throat.

Soon after, the minstrels start to play and everyone begins to dance. I tap my toe, sit forward in my seat. Edmund cocks one eye at the toe of my restless red shoe.

"I am not a dancing sort of man," he says with a half laugh. For the first time, I look at him properly.

He isn't old, middle twenties I am told, and he is good-looking in a rough, untrammelled sort of way. His clothes are costly but serviceable, no fur trim or satin sleeves for him. He wears his hair long; the light of the torches burnish it, revealing strands of red and copper. His upper lip is hidden by a vast moustache. As if he feels my eyes upon him, he turns to me and smiles again, a quick, uncertain smile, his eyes glinting green. He bows slightly. "But surely, my lady, you may have other partners."

I incline my head at his permission and shortly afterward take to the floor with Oliver. His familiar fingers are warm and his smile as mocking as it was in childhood, but there is no hostility now.

"So, our little Margaret is now the Countess of Richmond. Who would have thought it?"

I glance at him sideways.

"You for one, Oliver. Don't you recall suggesting I could be queen one day?"

He throws back his head and bellows with laughter, drawing all eyes upon us.

"I remember it well, little sister. We were in the garden. Poor John was quite taken with the idea too, as I recall."

My smile drops a little as I remember the innocence of those days. I had become accustomed to John. The idea of ruling him in such a way that a man hates to be ruled has not lost its appeal. I turn my gaze to the top table, where Edmund is quaffing another cup of wine. I cannot imagine any woman holding sway over him.

My chin drops, Oliver nudges me. "Hey," he says, "chin up. It won't be that hard. Edmund isn't a bad fellow ... for a Welshman."

The last is a joke, the sort typical of my brother, and I do my best to laugh, but the thought that a few hours from now I will be bedded down with a stranger, a man with whom I have exchanged no more than a few sentences, makes me sick to my stomach. I swallow my fear and take a deep breath, blow out my cheeks and stumble as I regain our place in the dance.

The music ceases.

"Another turn, my lady?" Oliver bows like a courtier but I see Mother summoning us and, still hand in hand, Oliver and I hurry toward her.

"Margaret," she says, ignoring her son and gathering me to her side. She inclines her head toward a young woman I have not met before. "This is Myfanwy. She lost her father recently and is travelling to join her uncle's household in Monmouth. She will be part of your company."

Myfanwy and I exchange shy smiles. She is a little older than me, or at least she is taller, stronger, and a deal more confident.

"I am pleased to meet you, my lady." She bobs a curtsey and when Mother waves us away, she chatters constantly as she follows me to my seat. Edmund and Jasper are conducting a loud and rather drunken argument about battle strategy. I raise my eyebrows at Myfanwy and she pulls a face in return – a face that expresses quite clearly her opinion of men when they are in their cups. I indicate the empty chair, urging her to sit. "Thank you," she murmurs as she comes to sit beside me.

As Myfanwy and I become acquainted the company grows tired. Ladies are hiding yawns behind their hands and men are sprawling in their chairs, belching quietly into their kerchiefs. Soon, the celebration will be over and it will be time to retire for the night.

My heart turns sickeningly. I cast a fearful look in the direction of my husband. He pushes back his chair, sways a little on his feet as he wags a finger at this brother to emphasise his final point of the argument. "Anyway, I am done with you," he barks. "I am off to my bed. Come wife!"

A great cheer goes up in the hall. Mother lifts her head. She promised me she would forbid any undue bawdry at our bedding time. To my great relief, the company makes no move to follow us, but they yell ignoble comments as I stand with shaking knees and let my husband engulf my hand with his.

His palm is calloused, his grip firm and unrelenting. I totter along behind him as he strides across the hall. As we pass, I cast a helpless glance over my shoulder at Mother, who refuses to look at me. She keeps her eyes firmly downcast but Oliver raises a hand, sends me a wave of both encouragement and pity. Myfanwy and Edith are standing together; both of them watching me go with something akin to horror. They are unwed, maidens both, yet they are more aware of what is to come than I.

At the top of the stairs, Edmund throws open the chamber door and I follow him inside. There is nothing untoward about the room; the fire is lit, the shutters drawn and candles are guttering beside the bed. At the hearth an elderly dog is slumbering, his brindle coat camouflaged in the flickering light.

I try not to look at the bed but I can see it from the corner of my eye. It is high and broad, the heavy drapes looped, the covers peeled back, revealing snow-white linen beneath. In a little while, I will be in that bed with this strange man. I have no idea how to act, what to say, or what to expect. I can only place my trust in God. I look about the room for somewhere to pray.

A timid knock comes at the door. At Edmund's curt reply, my woman pokes her head into the chamber. "We've come to help my lady make ready for the night."

He nods and moves toward the fireplace, slumps in a chair, his head in his hands.

The women speak in whispers, gently easing me from my clothes and placing them neatly on the press. The two youngest girls hold a sheet aloft so that I might discreetly wriggle from my shift and into my nightgown. Every so often I glance at Edmund who remains unmoving, staring into the flames, seemingly indifferent to my toilette. His hair shines gold in the firelight.

At last, I am ready. Too afraid to ask to be shown to the prie dieu, I am aided into the high chilly bed, where the covers are drawn up to my chin. Soon, my husband's servants will arrive to help him make ready and … God alone knows what will follow.

He does not move. The moments slip by, the coals glow red in the hearth and the dog snores gently. Close outside the window an owl calls.

I keep very still. With the covers clutched to my chin I watch him, lost in thought, at the hearth. It is as if he has forgotten all about me. I tell myself that if I hold my breath and keep silent, he will pass the night in his chair.

For a long time I wait, scarcely daring to breathe. When he finally moves, I jump and almost cry out in fright. He glances at me, gives a short laugh and begins to undo his sword belt.

I cannot look. I turn my head to his chair and watch as his garments fall one by one in a disarrayed heap; his sword, his jacket, his neckerchief. When he tosses off his jerkin, the silk lining shines bright and rich for a moment. Then, slowly, it slides from the seat onto the sleeping dog, who does not stir from his slumber.

As Edmund walks toward the bed, I keep my eyes averted. The mattress dips beneath his weight and I cling desperately to my side, terrified of rolling against him in his nakedness. His bare leg touches mine, and I draw away, my heart hammering, my chin beginning to tremble. Desperately, I begin a silent prayer. He reaches out, snuffs the candle, the bed curtain drops and we are cast into pitch darkness but there is little comfort in that.

My eyes are wide, staring into nothing. My throat is dry and tight. I want my mother. I want Edith. I wish with all my heart and soul that it was John lying beside me. John, who would be so easy to deny.

A great hand, warm and rough, settles on my knee. He squeezes, as if testing a mare for soundness. Then the bed ropes squeak as he bounces onto his back and lets out a loud, ungentlemanly yawn. He sighs again and shifts away from me, onto his side.

"Good night, Margaret," he says. "Sleep well; we have a long journey ahead on the morrow."

The Countess of Richmond

<u>The Road to Wales – 1455</u>

The family gather in the hall to bid me goodbye. I am allowed no time with Edith, and there can be no intimate discussion of what happened the night before. My husband wishes to make an early departure and, after a swift toilette and a swifter breakfast, I am helped onto my horse. More concerned with a loose thread upon her sleeve, Mother does not look at me as I ride away. But Edith is loath to see me go; she runs a little way after the cavalcade, her kerchief blowing in the chilly wind like a banner of surrender. She is the last person I see, and the last voice I hear is my brother Oliver, calling for me to have good cheer.

My throat is blocked with tears. I turn my face west, look toward Wales, thankful that we are riding into the wind and my tears may not be mistaken for sorrow. A horse moves up beside me, the stirrup leathers creaking.

"A long journey ahead, my lady." It is Myfanwy, her fresh face an insult to my shadowed eyes.

"Three days or more on the road, so my brother says," I reply. I find I am grateful for her presence. I am accompanied by my household women, but to me they seem elderly. Myfanwy's youth means I have at least the promise of a friend.

She smiles. "But they tell me the scenery is pretty."

I have rarely left the flooding, flat landscape of my birth. I miss the comfort of familiar wide vistas, and long stretching roads. Oliver says Wales is a land of clouds and rain, a mossy kingdom where sprites and spirits dwell. Usually, I would scorn such silly tales but today, riding away from everything I know and love, I fear they may be true.

Ahead of me, Edmund's broad back and that of his brother block my view, so I watch the roadside and see the familiar flat landscape fade into meadows and woodland.

We pass small hamlets where children with sacking on their shoulders to protect them from the weather stare blankly as we pass by. A girl of about my age chases a gaggle of geese into a farmyard. She turns and watches us, her hand to her brow, and I have the sudden urge to change places with her. I have no idea what it is to be an ordinary common girl, but given the chance, I would let her be the Countess of Richmond, riding into the unknown. I would happily become a goose-girl in this hamlet where nothing ever happens.

Mercifully, before I grow too tired, we break our journey at a wayside inn. Edmund helps me dismount, and as I stand stiffly, resisting the urge to rub my buttocks, I notice for the first time how long our cavalcade is.

We ride at the head to escape the worst of the dust and dirt, but behind are scores of carts and many people; soldiers and their followers, servants, cooks. There are supply wagons, and a litter for me should I grow too weary. As the falconer's cart pulls into the yard, I see that Edmund's elderly hound has taken refuge there, his head on his paws, watching the world with disinterest.

Myfanwy goes with me into the inn, the other women following behind, trying to hide their groans of discomfort after so long in the saddle. The interior is gloomy after the daylight ride and I blink to adjust my vision. It is a bleak place and the furnishings are rough but the brightly burning fire is welcome. As my women do all they can to ensure my comfort for an hour or two, I draw off my gloves and hold out my hands to the flames. I hadn't realised how chilled I had become.

"You'll get chilblains," Myfanwy warns as she comes to stand beside me. I ball my fists and, pull them from the warmth, turning to watch as refreshments are laid out on the table.

I am fed on cold meat, cheese and fresh baked bread; my thirst is quenched with warm, nutty ale. As my stomach fills I grow sleepy, and I greet Edmund's instruction to move on with an inward groan. All I want is to lie in a soft bed, but instead I must clamber back onto that horse. I wish I could refuse; I am tired of the saddle after just half a day, and it is likely to get so much worse.

"Shall I have the litter made ready?" Edmund asks and I realise he has noticed my fatigue. Unwilling that he should think me weak, I straighten my shoulders and stubbornly shake my head.

"No, no, thank you, I will ride. I am not an infant." I look about for a groom to help me mount, but Edmund is impatient. Without ceremony, he puts his hands about my waist, hoists me into the air as if I weigh nothing, and deposits me in the saddle. It is all I can do not to cry out as my tender delicate parts make contact with that dreaded seat.

"We stop at Oxford for the night, so make haste." He swings onto the back of his horse and at his command, the cavalcade moves forward with the hunting dogs running alongside. I turn my head toward the swaying curtains of the litter and wish with all my heart I was not so stubborn. A litter may not be the most comfortable mode of travel, but at least one can close one's eyes and be spared the relentless chaffing of the saddle.

At Oxford, the accommodation is cramped and I am spared any further intimacy with Edmund. He sleeps where he can with the other men, and Myfanwy shares my bed. I sleep soundly and wake refreshed, but in the morning I notice Edmund is heavy-eyed, his greeting terse. As the day wears on and we draw closer to our destination, the more he seems to brood. I wonder what I may have done to offend him.

By the time we approach the crossing into Wales, he is positively sulking. Myfanwy leans from her saddle to speak quietly. "What is the matter with your lord?" she asks. I shrug expressively. "I have no idea, but whatever it is I pray I am not the cause of it."

She shakes her head and smiles encouragingly as the horses begin to climb uphill. We pause on the ridge while Jasper points out the undulating land that betokens the Welsh border. As we grow closer, the rain begins, and by the time Caldicot Castle looms ahead, the road is swathed in mist and we are all drenched to the skin.

Caldicot Castle – November 1455

The household staff ride ahead to ensure all is in readiness for our arrival. We clatter through the towering gate, our arrival greeted by barking dogs and hovering, welcoming attendants. Edmund dismounts stiffly and throws his reins to a waiting groom. Then, to my surprise, he holds out a hand to me. I try to alight elegantly, but my back is aching and my thighs are sore. When my feet touch the ground, my knees give way, forcing me to clutch at his sleeve. His arms come out instantly, preventing me from falling, and he gives a wry smile, knowing my discomfort and finding it amusing.

"Welcome home, my lady." He bows and ushers me inside. Myfanwy follows, her cloak, as sodden as my own, bundled in her arms. She cranes her head to look about the hall, but I do not want to look. Overcome with a wave of bitter homesickness and exhaustion, I do not wish to find pleasure in anything I see. I am sure I will not be happy here, and hope against hope that we will not tarry long at Caldicot.

I follow Edmund into the hall where servants are scurrying around with trays of refreshment and two pages are wrestling a large chest through a narrow door. Edmund's dog takes up residence before the fire, the younger castle dogs giving ground to his authority. As we move toward the hearth, I struggle to untie the ribbon of my cloak but my fingers are cold and stiff, the sudden change in temperature making them burn painfully.

"Come here." Edmund stands before me. My face is level with his chest. As he fiddles with the ties, I inhale the scent of horses, ale, and rain. "There," he smiles. "All done."

My cloak slides from my shoulders and he offers me a cup. I drink gratefully, for I am thirsty from the road. "You must be hungry," he says, but I find I have little appetite. The things I crave most are a hot bath, fresh clothes, and a warm soft bed in which I can sleep for a week.

"I would like to go to my chamber first, if I may. I am tired and filthy from the road."

He puts down his cup and summons a servant. "Take my lady to the chamber and see to her comfort." I stand, beckon Myfanwy to follow, and try to conceal how strongly my legs and back protest at the movement.

My husband's apartments are well appointed, located on the upper floor of the gatehouse. Even on this dull day, the large windows allow plenty of light to stream into the room. While the maid orders water for a bath, I move to look out across the park. Myfanwy settles herself before the fireplace, where the leaping flames promise to soon warm even the furthest corners.

A manservant is stowing away Edmund's belongings, arranging his books on the table and setting his best boots to warm by the hearth. It is a comfortable chamber; well furnished with cushions and rugs, and sumptuous tapestries hanging on the walls. My husband has taste. When a servant enters with a tray of victuals, Myfanwy and I fall upon them as if we have been starved.

Tomorrow, Myfanwy is to travel on to Monmouth and I am loath to part with her. Her chatter prevented me from thinking, salving the wound in my heart where my family lodge. I am scared, ill at ease, and feel like a stranger in a strange country; a child in an adult world. There is no one in whom I can confide. In only a few days Myfanwy has become a real friend. She has in many ways replaced the confidant I once had in Edith. I have grown accustomed to her on our shared journey and will miss her when we part, as I miss them.

Just as the first tear drops from the end of my nose, a page arrives with a tub. I wipe my face with the back of my hand as a girl enters with a slopping pitcher of water. Soon, the promise of a warm bath chases some of the homesickness away. As the women line the tub with thick linen, Edmund's manservant makes a quiet, hasty exit. A procession of women, young and old, troop back and forth with buckets and jugs until the tub is full. Myfanwy helps me remove my damp kirtle and pull off my soiled stockings.

I soak up to my neck in warm water. The aches of the journey leach away and the grime seeps from my pores. My woman, Betony, washes my hair, rinsing it in an infusion of marigold and camomile. Afterwards, I sit before the bedchamber hearth while she tugs at the tangles. The fire warms me and, dressed in a loose gown, I am almost relaxed, almost sleepy.

And then Edmund comes. Betony leaps up from her knees and bobs a curtsey before fleeing. I wish I could follow her, take refuge with her in the steamy kitchens, but I am the countess, the lady of the house. My place is here. With him.

"Margaret, you are recovered from the ride?"

He sinks into a chair. His elderly wolfhound drops to the floor at his feet and looks up at me with big, soulful eyes. I reach out and click my fingers and the dog raises his head but does not move.

"What is his name?" I ask, for want of something better to say.

He laughs shortly. "Jasper."

"Jasper?" I cannot help but exclaim. I am astonished that he should give his dog the same name as his brother.

"But ... but ... what?"

"I was a boy when I named the pup, I thought it funny. I meant it as a jest, a friendly insult. My brother was furious, but I think he has forgiven me now. We call him Jay these days – to distinguish the two."

I can feel a giggle brewing. I bite my lip but he can see the laughter in my eyes. He leans forward and caresses the dog's silky ear.

"He is an old fellow now, nearing the end of his days. I will miss him."

Jasper, or Jay as I must remember to call him, thumps his tail on the rush matting, his expression pathetic as if he can understand every word and mourns his own imminent demise.

Edmund nods to his page to fill two cups with wine and bring them to the fireside. "You can go now," he orders and the fellow makes his escape, leaving us alone.

There is nothing to say. We sit sipping wine in silence. The logs shift and crackle in the hearth and outside the wind howls about the tower. On this wild winter's night I am safe indoors, but I don't feel it. I am ill at ease and awkward.

I wish I was wearing more than this loose gown that is too wide at the neck for decency, the short wide sleeves showing my bare arms. I wish my hair was pulled tight beneath a wimple, instead of falling free and fluffy beneath my white linen cap. Edmund stretches out his legs, crosses his ankles and balances his cup on his chest.

"You are very young, Margaret."

His gaze is steady, unsettling.

"I am thirteen."

He snorts and takes another slurp of wine.

"I would you were older. I need a wife. I need to be a husband not a nurse maid."

I bridle, unable to conceal my annoyance.

"I need no nurse maid, Sir."

He laughs at my tight lips, and sits up to lean toward me, his forearms resting on his knees, but he does not look at me direct. He swirls the wine in the bottom of his cup and when he speaks, his voice is earnest.

"I am not a brute, my lady. I would things were different, but I cannot change fate. I cannot make you older, and neither can I wait for you to grow up. I must get myself a son."

My face burns. He should not speak of these things. I duck my head, chin to my chest, and wonder what Mother would have me say.

I am worldly-wise enough to know he needs a son to secure my fortune; my properties will not be his until I produce a child. My heart thumps and dread surges in my belly as I recall the awful things Oliver told me about reproduction. I have seen the dogs in the castle rutting where they can, and the memory fills me with revulsion that I should be expected to take part in such an act. As the silence grows, I try to remember everything my mother tried to teach me about obedience, about my position, my duty. I do not answer him and he grows angry.

Wine slops to the floor as he slumps back in his chair.

"Go to bed," he growls and at his dismissal, I leap to my feet and scurry to do his bidding.

It is dark in the bedchamber, the candles almost spent and the embers dying in the hearth. A chill draught blows in beneath the door. This would never have been allowed to happen at home. I long for the warm comfort of my nursery, the bed I shared with Edith, Agnes, and Elizabeth. With a sob of homesickness, I dive beneath the covers, draw my knees to my chin and try very hard not to cry. Soon the pillow grows damp, my nose blocks with snot and my eyes smart. A short time later, when the door opens and a shaft of light falls across the bed, I realise I have forgotten my prayers.

I hear the thud of Edmund's boots as they hit the floor, the clank of his discarded sword belt. I hear his garments fall one by one and then the mattress sinks beneath his weight.

With my back to him, I shut my eyes tight, breathe long and slow, trying to pretend I am sleeping. He rolls against me, his arms slide up around my body, his fingers fumble at the neck of my shift.

I cannot allow this. I cannot let it happen. When I dare to speak, my voice is muffled by the blankets.

"My mother said you wouldn't bed me until I was of an age."

He rolls me onto my back.

"Your mother lied."

I cannot see him clearly; he is but a shadow, a monster in the dark. His breath is foul with wine and, to my horror, I realise he is drunk.

"She wouldn't have married me to you had she known."

"Your mother would have married you to the devil for the right fee."

I am silenced. Remembering a thousand instances when I had doubted her, I fight and fail to disbelieve his wicked lie. When he begins to lift my shift, my body turns rigid. I jump when his hot, searching fingers touch upon my skin, his lips, tentative at first, are wet upon my neck. I sob and bite my lip, closing my eyes tight, straining away from him.

I can speak of this no more ...

The next morning, my women tut-tut at the bruises on my thigh. Betony creeps around, makes soothing noises as she washes me, her hands gentle. Every so often she glances at me as if fearful I may break. I stare at the ceiling and wish I had never been born.

To my relief, Edmund rides out early with his troop, leaving me free to wander the castle. Before she takes her leave, Myfanwy and I walk in the small garden. The earth is dormant and we tiptoe through sprawling dead nettles and fallen leaves.

"Can I write to you, Margaret? I have so enjoyed our short time together."

I reach out and take her hand, trying not to cling to it.

"Please do, I shall like that."

We pass a little farther along the path, careful not to slip on the wet leaves. When we reach the boundary we look out across the moat, and I sense her heart is as heavy as my own.

"Margaret." She slides her arm around my shoulder as if she is an elderly aunt. "Things will get better; it won't always feel like this..."

I stiffen. I had hoped to keep my misery a secret. "Of course, I know nothing of these things," she continues. "But I have overheard enough to believe that, after the first time, it is easier. The pain will-"

"Myfanwy!" I am sharp. I close my eyes take a breath to calm my embarrassment and speak through clenched teeth. "I do not wish to speak of it." I shrug my shoulders, pretending nonchalance. "It is just another duty I must bear."

She relaxes. She has believed my lie, my self-delusion.

"And when your child comes, it will all be worthwhile."

"Yes."

I look down at my flat chest, my narrow unfruitful hips, and wonder how that can ever be.

Rashly, I promise to invite her to Caldicot for a visit as soon as she is properly settled, and then we embrace and she is helped onto her horse. She rides unhappily away. Monmouth is not so far, but too far for weekly visits. From now on, we will meet only seldom

I climb to the top of one of the towers and watch her go. She turns regularly in her saddle to acknowledge the salute of my floating kerchief. When she turns no more, I sink to my knees, and behind the shelter of the battlement, give way to tears. I am a sorry, wretched child deprived of a playmate. When I can weep no more I linger on the tower, alone beneath the wide, grey sky.

I cannot stay up there forever, and as rain begins to fall I take refuge in our apartments, where a fire is roaring and the victual table is laden with food. I have no appetite but to please my women, I nibble an apple and a piece of cheese.

I cannot seem to dispel my low spirits. If Mother were here she would insist I take up my needlework or go for a long, brisk walk. But she isn't here, so I draw my knees up beneath my skirts, stare into the heat of the flames and wallow in idleness.

A stealthy sound draws me from sleep. I wipe a trickle of drool from my chin and scramble to my feet. Edmund is home, rainwater dripping from his cloak onto the floor. My body stiffens as he takes it off and throws it at his page. As the boy leaves the room, Edmund moves to the fire and holds out his hands to the flames.

"It is turning colder," he says over his shoulder. "I wouldn't be surprised if we are in for some early snow."

I don't want that. Snow would prolong our stay here. Snow would keep Myfanwy and I apart for longer. Snow, if it were bad enough, might even prevent Edmund from riding out every day.

Realising I am standing like a statue in front of my chair, I give myself a mental shake and remember my careful training.

"Can I order you refreshment? Shall I call somebody?"

"Nay, you can pour me a cup but leave them. I hate servants under my feet all the time."

I move to the table and watch the thick red liquid cascade into the cup. Then, without standing too close, I hand it to him.

"Thank you." He raises the cup before quaffing it. He smacks his lips and pulls up a chair. "Sit, sit," he orders. "Tell me of your day."

I am startled, my mind quite suddenly blank. How have I spent my day? I clear my throat.

"I walked in the gardens. Myfanwy rode to join her uncle in Monmouth." I fall silent. In truth, after she left, my day deteriorated into misery, but I cannot tell him that.

"You'll miss her?" He leans forward in his seat, our eyes meet. My gaze falls away first.

"Yes, I will. I haven't known her long, yet ... she quickly became a friend."

He is watching me, his eyes narrowed. I am not sure if he is angry, or merely thinking. He makes a sudden movement, slaps his knee.

"Then call her back. Give her a place in your household."

I open my eyes wide. I have never engaged my own staff but I am quite certain my ladies have been selected from only good stock. Myfanwy is respectable, but her bloodline is wanting.

"Is she...? Can I...? Myfanwy is - "

Edmund interrupts me. "Listen, Margaret. We are not at Bletsoe now. You no longer have to live beneath the jurisdiction of your mother. You are the Countess of Richmond and answer only to me. You are lonely and lack a friend. I say that, within reason, you can do as you please."

He looks satisfied, almost smug, as if he is scoring points against my mother. I realise, quite suddenly, that he doesn't like her. I wonder why.

"Really? I can do as I please? Order my own household, my own entertainments and diversions?"

He throws back his head and laughs, showing strong yellow teeth. He looks different when he is happy; the threat is gone, or at least the danger is less apparent. When he sobers, he reaches over and takes my hand. I refrain from snatching it away. He fiddles with my fingers, feeling the birdlike structure of my bones.

"I want you to be happy, Margaret. As long as you don't sleep with my grooms, you can do as you please. I have to have an heir. Just give me a son and I will give you the moon if you want it."

I am overwhelmed. To give him a son, the act I endured last night will need to be repeated over and over, and there are no guarantees that I am old enough to conceive. Yet his last words are the kindest ever spoken to me. I turn away and look at the passing day outside the casement, scudding clouds in a blue-pink sky.

"Whatever would I do with the moon?" I ask, and he subsides into laughter again.

Caldicot Castle - March 1456

A few months later Myfanwy rides back to Caldicot. She tumbles from her horse and into my arms.

"Oh Margaret! I am so pleased to be here. My aunt is livid, of course, at having lost a free servant, but my uncle was glad to see the back of me. He already has enough mouths to feed and had no hesitation in letting me know it. Oh, we will have such fun now."

She is like a breath of summer wind on a winter's day, making my cheeks warm and my lips turn upward. Arm in arm, we hurry into the comfort of the hall and up to my favourite chamber. On the way, she chatters non-stop, filling the worried corners of my mind with nonsense. Despite everything, despite my aching limbs and the knowledge that it will soon be night again, I feel my spirits rise.

Myfanwy doesn't realise she hasn't yet allowed me a chance to speak. She removes her cloak and draws her gloves from long slim fingers, readjusts her wimple.

"We can get to work on the tapestry you were planning now. I have my work basket with me. When I was young, my stepmother taught me all the finest stitches ..." She stops, suddenly realising my silence, noticing my pale face. "Are you well, Margaret? "

"I am now," I reply quietly, and draw her to the settle. "You were right. Things have got better. I am growing accustomed to my husband and slowly finding my feet here at Caldicot."

My words are not entirely truthful but she smiles her pleasure. "I am glad. Will this be your permanent home, or will you visit your husband's other holdings?"

Edmund has vast estates, both in Wales and England, all of which require an army of lawyers to deal with the administration.

"I expect we will visit all in turn. I know he plans to move on to Lamphey soon; he says it is an easier base from which to soothe the unrest."

After my uncle's death at St Albans, the Welsh castles were granted to York, but local Welshman Gruffydd ap Nicholas and his henchmen, resent both York's power and Edmund's presence in Wales. The Welshman is causing trouble; speaking out against the protectorate, refusing to surrender his castles, and Edmund has no option but to move against him.

From his conversations with Jasper I have gleaned that Edmund intends to do his duty by the king. First to enforce the payment of ap Nicholas's debt to the crown, and weaken his position by taking the castles he has in his possession. The castles in question have strange sounding names: Aberystwyth, Carreg Cenen, Carmarthen, and Cydweli. I try out the words in the privacy of my chamber and wonder if they will ever trip easily from my tongue. But I have no wish to speak politics with Myfanwy; she is here to divert me from my troubles. I make light of the situation and turn my attention to more domestic matters.

"These may be dangerous times, Myfanwy, but we are safe enough here in Caldicot."

"It is a pretty castle. I thought so today as I rode toward it; it was like a home coming." She gets up and pushes open the casement letting in a blast of cold air. She leans out. "We should do something about the gardens – they are in a sorry state. If you set men to work on them now, come summer you will reap the rewards."

It is a good idea. Her enthusiasm is contagious and I join her at the window.

"We can grow herbs and concoct remedies. I know all about it. I spent many hours in the still-room at Bletsoe. I wonder why I didn't think of it myself."

"We must make a list!" Myfanwy scrambles up and goes to fetch a quill and parchment.

While Edmund sets out to quell the unruly Welsh, Myfanwy and I put all our efforts into the new physic garden. My domesticity is punctuated by couriers who come and go at all hours, bearing messages between my husband and his allies. To my relief, these matters keep Edmund up long into the night, while he perfects his strategy. By the time he comes to bed, he is often too tired to do more than take off his outer clothes and fall onto the pillow beside me, leaving me listening to his snores as I try to drift off to sleep again.

In the morning, he is up before the lark. I open my eyes just as he is leaving, bid him farewell and then sink back into my dreams. I am sleeping well now, rising late and eating heartily; the long hours in the fresh air giving me the appetite of a growing boy.

I grow accustomed to life at Caldicot. I no longer dwell on my life at Bletsoe or spend hours wondering what Edith and Elizabeth are doing. The castle inhabitants grow used to me, too. When I pass along the corridors, the servants smile before they lower their heads and move out of my path. The cook sends tasty morsels to my table, with the message that the dish was made especially with me in mind. With Edmund's support, one by one, the women that came with me from my mother's house return to England, to be replaced with younger, brighter companions. These new women are my choice, local women loyal to me, and I am satisfied that they will not bear tales back to Bletsoe. My letters to Mother, Edith and Oliver bear all the news I wish them to have of me.

I find my feelings toward my mother have altered. Edmund insists she was aware the marriage would be consummated, aware of his need for a son. I remember how she refused to look at me on my wedding night, or the morning after when I rode away, and the suspicion grows that Edmund is telling the truth. She lied to me, sending me blindly to my fate. The knowledge hurts, and I am not sure I can forgive her. I have little wish to look upon her again.

Of course, the unspoken question on everyone's lips is of my condition. Mother is bold enough to send letters, asking me outright if I have reason to suspect a pregnancy. I do not answer, but her enquiry tells me one thing. I know she lied to me. Had she made it a condition of our wedding that I was to be left intact, she would not be asking. I realise now that Mother's concern has always been more for what she can gain from my marriage rather than for my happiness.

To my surprise, I am not unhappy in Wales. I miss my siblings, but there are compensations. I am mistress of my own affairs, surrounded by friends, and the garden keeps me busy from dawn 'til dusk.

Outside of the bedroom, my husband's demands are not unreasonable, and even after he snuffs out the last candle, he is as considerate as he can be, ensuring the matter is not prolonged. Afterwards, he dries my tears and cuddles me, promising treats and gifts in way of reparation. In many ways it is as if I am his treasured child and not his dutiful spouse.

I have begun to blossom. At last my breasts are developing and my courses, that were previously sporadic, now come regularly. I am growing up at last but, regrettably, not into a beauty.

My face is still too long and thin, and I doubt that will ever change. Betony shows me how to use padding beneath my gowns to emphasise my breasts and round out my flat, boyish hips. I order the most sumptuous gowns I can afford, and shoes, lots of shoes, with heels to make me taller, fashioned by the best craftsmen in the most pliant leather to be found. Almost daily parcels are delivered; new clothes or jewels that swamp my tiny frame with lustre.

My women laugh as they adorn me in my latest acquisition. A blood-red velvet gown with hanging sleeves, lined with the softest miniver. Tonight, Jasper is dining with us. Lately returned from court, he is staying for a few days while he and his brother discuss local strategy.

To Myfanwy's joy, I have insisted she accompany me as my attendant, and she too dresses with special care. She is fairer by far than I, and I always think it a shame to see her honey-coloured hair tucked from sight beneath her wimple. Tonight, she is dressed in a deep yellow gown, an old one of mine that she has let out and added new sleeves. She looks as much the lady as I, and I know my mother would scold me for allowing her to step above her station. But any guilt I may feel vanishes when Myfanwy turns to me, her eyes shining, and holds out her arms.

"How do I look?"

"Beautiful." I reply without hesitation, because there is no other honest reply I can make.

"And so do you." She takes my arm and we stand side by side before the glass. I see the contrast. My body is slight beside her roundness and my face long against her pink plump radiance and know she doesn't speak the truth. But I pat her hand before turning away from my reflection.

It is sinful to wish for beauty that God hasn't seen fit to provide me with; there are far greater gifts I should be seeking, such as generosity, piety, compassion, kindness. But I suppose, if the truth be told, a longing for loveliness is common to all women.

When Myfanwy and I enter the hall, curious heads turn our way. The hubbub of excitement dips a little as we take our seats. Sweet smelling herbs have been dispersed to ensure the hall is fresh, and dried petals, like a scattering of summer memories, lie strewn upon the table.

Edmund and Jasper are already in their places, cups in hand, their heads together in conversation. Music begins, discordant at first, and the two men stop talking to acknowledge our arrival. Jasper, after a start of surprise, rises to his feet, bows and ushers us to our chairs, while Edmund leans back in his seat. I can almost feel Myfanwy's excitement as she looks upon her first banquet. Her face is glowing, her eyes dancing. Jasper summons a servant to fill our cups, his eyes faltering as he absorbs Myfanwy's creamy skin. He barely glances at me before turning back to Edmund.

It is good to forget war for a while, and I am glad when the men turn their minds from their joint campaign. Jasper, younger and more gallant than Edmund, leads both myself and Myfanwy onto the floor. He is surprisingly light of foot; a man altogether more socially aware than his brother, who is more at home in the saddle than in company. I have the last dance with Jasper and when he leads me back to my seat, Edmund is waiting. He bids me sit beside him, apologising as he always does, that he is not a dancing man.

It is a night of cheer. The company is replete with food and wine, and dawn is almost upon us when we finally go in search of our beds. I am the first to crumble and give in to fatigue. Jasper is about to lead me onto the floor again when Edmund sees me hide a yawn behind my hand. He laughs gently and gets to his feet, firmly retrieving me from his brother.

"It is bedtime, wife," he says, relieving Jasper of my hand. I turn to wish my brother-in-law good night, and he bows over my wrist. Then, to her delight, he pays Myfanwy the same compliment.

As Edmund leads me away and Myfanwy reluctantly follows, I see her cheeks have turned quite pink. Jasper, gently swaying on his feet, watches us go with a half-smile on his face, before turning in the direction of the guest chambers.

Upstairs, the room is warm, the bedcovers turned back and welcoming. Myfanwy follows us into the apartment but Edmund holds out an arm. "Margaret will not need you tonight."

Startled, Myfanwy looks from him to me and back again, her eyes wide and questioning. Then, quite helpless in the face of my husband's authority, she dips a curtsey and bids us goodnight.

"Goodnight," I whisper as I stand looking into the flames. My mind is teeming with images, my head muzzy with wine, and too much food lies in my belly. I undo my girdle and place it on the table, pull off my hennin and veil, letting my hair fall free. "I am tired," I say. "It was a good night."

Edmund sits on the edge of the bed and tries to kick off his boots. The wine he has drunk makes him fumble so I kneel before him, pull them off one by one and cast them into the corner. He wiggles his toes and leans back, watching me.

"You dance very well. Very… elegantly."

I am startled. He has never paid me a compliment before. I shake my head depreciatively, unused to such niceties.

"There are much more elegant ladies than I."

I can feel the blood flooding, hot beneath my skin so I keep my head turned, my eyes on the floor. He reaches out, a finger beneath my chin and forces me to look at him.

"Let me be the judge." He winks and I blush all the harder, but do not resist when he pulls me closer and begins to unlace the back of my gown.

As usual he is gone by the time I wake. I slide from the mattress, and gathering the sheet about my naked body, I go to the window. A promise of spring is in the air, a cold brisk breeze making the catkins dance, a few brave primroses peeking from beneath decaying leaves.

Myfanwy and I have expanded our plans for the garden. I have ordered a fountain to be made, and sent abroad for roses, lavender and columbine. Edmund warns me they may not thrive here where it is so wet and chill, but the desire to try negates his wisdom.

I shiver a little as the air whispers against my bare shoulder. If anyone should see me, naked and as brazen as a dockside whore, there would be a scandal. Knowing my women will arrive at any moment, I reach out to pull the casement closed but a movement in the garden draws my eye. I glimpse the shade of Myfanwy's favourite gown and lower my arm to watch.

She is walking with Jasper, her fingers tucked in the crook of his arm. He seems to be addressing her as if she is his equal. As I watch, she turns her face from him, her eyes downcast. He is speaking rapidly, earnestly, and her confusion is evident even at this distance. She shakes her head, bites her lip and turns back to him.

I do not need to hear his words to realise I am witnessing a courtship. But, with her status so far beneath his, Myfanwy can only be courting disaster.

I frown and pull the window quietly closed. After pondering the matter throughout my morning toilette, I decide to say nothing. What can I say that would not alienate her? Instead, I concentrate on the garden; dwell upon which colours I should use for the altar piece I am embroidering for our chapel.

On her return, Myfanwy is quiet, as if lost in turbulent thoughts. I am careful not to pry into her mind. There are things it is better not to know but ... if she were to get with child, the scandal would touch me. I bite my lip, uncertain what I should do, or whom I should turn to for advice. As Countess of Richmond, I am her guardian as well as her friend, and Edmund would be furious were she to bring scandal upon me. I cannot even contemplate what my mother would say should the matter come to her ears.

Yet, while Edmund continues to ride about the countryside in the king's name, I stay quietly at home, minding my business, and only the promise of the coming spring keeps me steady.

Several times a day I gravitate toward to the small stone chapel where I pray, beseeching God to send me a son. With a child in my belly, Edmund will leave me in peace. He has promised me this. Although I know that one day he will desire more children, the thing I long for most is a reprieve from his attentions.

I am accustomed to the act of coupling now; there is no pain, just a sort of repugnance. It is a mystery to me why such store is set on love when it is such an inelegant thing. I cannot reconcile the emotions the minstrels sing of so plaintively with the act Edmund subjects me to. There is no beauty in it; no gentle touching of souls. It is embarrassing and rather smelly. For all his tender murmurings, designed to make me welcome him, once the joining is over, I feel like a brood mare, or a prize cow selected for service to produce the fattest calf.

But, to my joy, by the end of April, I fall sick and he spares me his nightly attention. At first, I fear I have contracted some ailment; I throw up every morning and the thought of food revolts me. But when my women notice my breasts are beginning to swell and are tender to the touch, they cast up their hands with joy and confirm my suspicion. I am, at last, with child. When I break the news to Edmund, he is more than delighted. He falls to his knees before me, spans my still flat belly with his big, calloused hands.

"God bless you, Margaret. I swear you will not be sorry. I will honour you for ever more."

He is such a child in his joy that I place my hands on his copper-gold hair and am almost stirred into affection. Perhaps this child we share will bring us closer, make us happy. I pray it will be so.

Summer is very welcome. The sketchy plans Myfanwy and I made in the early spring are now coming to fruition. The paths are clearly marked, the flower beds have been dug deeply and thoroughly manured, and cartloads of plants begin to arrive. We collect snips and cuttings from the hedgerow, request shoots from nearby gardens. Soon the herbs will begin to flourish and we can collect the leaves and dry them in the still-room to provide comfort and relief from winter colds and other ailments.

Even in a small castle like Caldicot, the inhabitants welcome a little cosseting when they are ill. There are always minor accidents, cuts and bruises, boils and wens, tooth ache, belly upsets; and there are women's problems aplenty that can be soothed with a well brewed posset. After the ignorant rough handling of their fellows, they will be glad of a knowledgeable hand to aid them.

As the spring flowers come into bloom, Myfanwy and a few others of my household begin sneezing, their noses red and running. At first, I suspect a summer cold but Myfanwy shakes her head.

"Don't worry, my lady," she says, dabbing at her nose again. "It is the same every year as the flowers begin to bloom – my stepmother called it the Summer Ague and dosed me with feverfew and eyebright." She nods toward the immature plants at her feet. "But it seems I will have to wait awhile."

She stoops to pluck a snail from a fresh green leaf, holding it gingerly between finger and thumb. "My stepbrothers used to stamp on them but I can never bring myself to do so." She hurls the creature over the wall, wipes her fingers on her apron and we move along the path, pointing out gaps in the planting and discussing what best to grow there.

"Of course, by the summer there won't be room to move, everything will be twice as big as it is now. It is best to pick leaves constantly, keep the plants contained. Old leaves are good for nothing anyway ..."

She stops suddenly and I cock my ear to raised voices coming from the other side of the wall. A clarion blasts and the sound of hooves thunder. With one accord we abandon the garden, lifting our skirts to hasten our steps. We duck our heads beneath the low doorway into the bailey, and are met with chaos.

The castle dogs are barking, men are shouting as heavily burdened servants dodge through a bevy of wild-eyed horses. Mail-clad men issue orders that no one seems to follow. I scan the melee for Edmund, but he is nowhere to be seen. A boy runs past, forgetting to acknowledge me. I grab for his sleeve but too late ... the stuff of his sleeve slips from my grasp and he is gone, disappearing down the steps to the under croft.

"What has happened? Where is your master?" I call to one of Edmund's guards who is battling with his harness. He pulls himself upright, and throws back his mailed hood, his hair clinging wetly to his head. He turns exhausted eyes upon me.

"He is with the injured, Madam, I should think. In the hall ..." He waves an arm in the direction of the steps and slumps onto a nearby wall.

My stomach churns.

"Thank you," I murmur as I hurry in search of my husband, fearful of what I will find. I turn feverish with horror. Edmund is injured? How? When? Why did this happen?

As we run up the stone steps and into the gloom of the great hall, I am aware of Myfanwy's tread echoing mine.

I scan the room, searching for Edmund, but he is just one man, lost in a crowd of groaning injured. The wounded have been laid out in a long, long line. One man, his head almost in the hearth, is calling for water; another, his face as white as a winding sheet, lies silent, his eyes closed, to all intents and purposes dead. I mutter a prayer as I frantically search for Edmund.

I stumble; a torn banner is wrapped around one of the wounded. As I pass, he grips my ankle, cries out for water. His hose is ripped, his tunic blood soaked. Beside me, Myfanwy's face is a mask of horror. I realise I must cast my own concerns aside.

"Fetch help." I lift my skirts and kneel beside the boy. "Bring as many women as you can, Myfanwy, and linen for bandages, and salve. Hurry!"

She jerks awake, nods just once, and flees the room. My duty as countess battles with my duty to my husband, who maybe lies just feet away. Even now he could be sucking in his last breath. I slide my hand beneath the boy's head.

"It is all right now. You are safe. I will take care of you."

I feel awkward. I am no nurse and unused to the sickroom, a stranger to battle wounds. I have only ever dealt with splinters and grazes, while the wounds around me are deep and wide. The boy whimpers, licks his lips. He can be no older than me. I think of his mother, the years he has left; the things he has yet to do; the joys he has yet to know. Yet there is only me standing between him and death. His head flops on my arm, and he opens his eyes and moans.

"It hurts."

"I know, I know, but God is with us. Be brave, remember to breathe and all will be well."

What nonsense I speak! There is an arrow lodged in his breast, his life's blood is dwindling, and I lack the knowledge to tend him. I glance up the hall to where Jasper is staunching blood, tearing strips of linen, feverishly binding wounds and tipping water down parched throats; water that might be as fatal as their wounds. Close by, a priest is praying. The droning comfort of his Latin verses add calm to a world turned cruel and bloody.

"Jasper," I scream. "Where is Edmund?" And then my husband stands up and looks down at the man he has been tending, dithering as to which man to aid next. Relief floods through me. He is tall, unmarred, and blessedly alive.

"Edmund," I whisper. "Thank God." And he turns and hurries toward my voice.

"Margaret, this is no place for you. Go back to your apartment ..."

I look down at the soldier at my feet.

"This one is just a boy. We must help him."

He strides forward, pushes me out of the way and touches the boy's cheek.

"Ned. Take heart, boy."

I cannot take my eyes from my husband. He is detached, business-like and efficient, but I realise he knows the lad's name, probably knows the name of every man in his troop. Edmund is that sort of leader. He is a good man and his household love him. They would follow him to the ends of the Earth. I had not realised that before.

"Now is not to the time to die," he says as he tears the boy's tunic open. Ned tries to smile, fails, his eye rolling, and Edmund, in desperation, calls for assistance just as Myfanwy appears. Her breath is ragged, her cheeks flushed and dirt-streaked. She thrusts a bundle of sheets at me and I begin ripping them into strips, my small hands made strong by need.

"It will hurt, lad, but it must be done," Edmund says. "You bite on this and think of your sweetheart, or your mother."

He thrusts the handle of his dagger between the patient's teeth and with a swift, gentle motion sweeps the sweaty hair from the boy's forehead. He looks at me. "Have some wadding ready, Margaret."

I nod determinedly.

Then, the bulk of his body shielding me from his actions, he gets to work. Myfanwy sits on Ned's legs, uttering soothing sounds while I bite my lip and silently pray. The boy's screams are loud and long, his knees twisting in agony, his fingers like claws. This is beyond me; I swallow vomit, try to keep breathing and beseech God to show mercy. I shift just a little to afford myself a better view, although it is probably better not to look. Edmund grips the shaft of the arrow, grunts with exertion, grimacing with the distaste of his task. Then, with a jerk, the boy falls back in a dead faint. His skin turns rapidly grey, his lips tinged with blue. He lies so still I fear he has stopped breathing.

"Quick." Edmund holds out a hand. I thrust the wadding and rolled bandages toward him and he works swiftly to bind the wound. "Hold that there, press hard." I do as I am bid, the linen turning scarlet, staining my fingers as I instruct my rebellious stomach not to weaken. The boy cannot possibly live after losing so much blood.

Moments pass in silence while Edmund hastily ties a bandage to hold the wadding in place.

"What happened?" I ask at last, turning to look at my husband properly for the first time this afternoon. His face is pale, daubed with dirt and gore, and there is a deep cut on his chin. Otherwise, he seems unharmed.

"They came upon us unawares. We were almost home; the boys were singing, riding loose in their saddles, looking forward to the feast. Damn me for a fool that I let it happen ..."

"But who attacked you?"

"ap Nicholas. He is a damnation, a thorn in my flesh, but I will have him soon. He will not find me unguarded a second time, I promise you that."

Edmund stands up and looks grimly about the room, hands on hips, his face desolate. "There are about twenty injured but, praise be, we have lost only one ... so far."

Order is swiftly returning; the wounded are quieter now they are well attended. The castle women provide ease, the priest gives spiritual comfort. Soon, the most able of the wounded will be carried off to their quarters. The boy, Ned, snores, his head thrown back in oblivion. Survival is up to him now.

Edmund holds out a hand and I grasp it, allow him to pull me from my knees. I look down at my ruined gown, brush away some of the filth and make a face.

"I must go and change. I will order a bath drawn for you, Edmund, and perhaps we should dine quietly in our chamber this evening. The men need to rest. This is no time for feasting."

He tries to smile but his eyes are bleak. I realise he is still holding my hand.

"I will come with you, wife," he says, and as if he is a small, tired boy, I lead him to our chamber.

Once closeted in our private chamber we do not speak. He slumps in a chair. Ignoring my soiled, bloodstained gown, I kneel before him and begin to pull off his boots. His head lolls, his red hair damp upon his forehead, his cheeks thick with dirt.

"I shall call for water so you can wash," I say, using his knee as an aid to help me rise. As I make to move away, he grabs for my hand, detaining me. I look down at his big fingers encircling my narrow wrist.

"You worked well, Margaret. Thank you."

Our eyes meet, and through the grime I notice a glimmer of something, the beginnings of camaraderie perhaps. I feel blood rush to my cheeks, drag my eyes from his. I shrug, trying to hide my pleasure.

"It was my duty as your wife and countess to help in any way I could. I only wish - "

"Shh, you were not wanting in any way, and I thank you for it."

Unable to help myself, I smile again. His grip releases me, but as I make to move away, his voice halts me again. "I was bringing you a gift but I fear it may not have survived the turmoil. Bring me my coat."

With great curiosity, I drag his coat from beneath the pile of belongings heaped in the corner and place it on his knee. With an unreadable look, he plunges his fist into one of the deep pockets and begins to draw something from it.

"Wait, turn around; don't look yet."

I am bursting to know what he has concealed, but obediently I turn away, closing my eyes and placing my hands over my face to make sure I do not weaken and peek.

"Ah," he says. "Thank goodness. I thought you might have perished, little chap. Here, Margaret, see if you can save him. He is one of a litter of seven the stable lad found abandoned in the barn. The rest have perished. I thought he might salve your sadness."

My hands drop from my face and I spin round to see a tiny kitten, surely too young to be taken from its mother. It balances in the palm of his hand, a scrap of tabby fur with blue weeping eyes. Instinctively, I reach for it, raise him to eye level. The poor thing can barely hold his head aloft.

I look at my husband who is, in turn, watching me. "I fear I cannot save him, Edmund, but I will do my best."

"You always do, my dear. Don't think it has gone unnoticed."

Wearily, he rests his head back again and closes his eyes. I tiptoe to the door in search of sustenance for the poor mite now clasped to my bosom, but as I reach the threshold, I pause and turn toward him again.

"Edmund," I say with great daring, disturbing his rest. "I should like you to know I am no longer sad. I am beginning to enjoy my life here and I am looking forward to our future and the birth of our son with great … joy, and pride."

Then, before he can fully open his eyes, I flee in the direction of the kitchen, calling for Myfanwy as I go.

For a few days, beneath our continuous ministrations, the kitten appears to thrive, but then, I awake one morning and find him stiff and cold on my counterpane. My bitter weeping penetrates Edmund's sleep and he stirs, sits bolt upright to discover what ails me. His hand is gentle on my shoulder as we look down at the tiny stiff body. "Come Margaret, do not weep. It's just a kitten."

I smear salty moisture across my cheeks with the back of my hand and blink up at him. I try to speak but my voice goes awry, my face distorts and more tears gather. With one movement he sweeps me into his arms, lies me back on the pillow and, tucking the covers around us both, gathers me to lie against him.

"No more weeping, Margaret. Forget the kitten, I wish I had not brought him to you. Let us dwell upon our son."

He begins to speak of the astonishing child that will soon be born to us, and as he does so, he plays with the ends of my hair. I can hear his voice rumbling in his chest, smell the aroma of his body with which I am now familiar. It is all strangely comforting. I relax against him, finding relief in his presence as he draws my thoughts away from the tragedy of the kitten to the miracle of our unborn child.

Caldicot Castle – July 1456

The boy Ned, who was so badly injured, is recovering slowly. I have taken him into my household, where he is learning the skills of a houseboy. He is quick to learn, and Jay has taken an unexpected liking to him; he spends his waking hours in the boy's company while his master is away.

Edmund's task to overcome ap Nicholas has become a quest. He is like a man driven; up at first light and awake until the following dawn he allows himself no ease. Sometimes I do not see him for a week; sometimes he is gone but half a day. In July, he stays at the Bishop's Palace at Lamphey for a month, and then arrives home unexpectedly.

I am in the garden, which has become my favourite retreat. In my hand is a letter from my sister Edith, who writes of her forth-coming marriage, her hopes for the future. My life at Bletsoe is remote now, the everyday household matters of little concern to me. I hope Mother has found Edith a good man with whom she will be happy. I let the letter drop and look about me.

The plants are burgeoning, some of them out of control. The roses sprawl with marigolds and camomile, their fragrance almost overpowering. I have been gathering flowerheads, and my lap is full of aromatic colour.

Jay comes lumbering into the garden first; he shoves his wet nose into my hand, insisting I pet him. His head is as soft as silk, the bones of his skull easily discernible beneath. I stare into his dark sad eyes and in response, his tail thumps on the path, raising dust. I hear a footstep and when I look up I find Ned hovering nervously, his cap in his hand. "The Earl and his troop are approaching the castle, my lady," he tells me, a commotion in the bailey confirming his announcement.

Edmund is home.

I leap to my feet, orange petals scattering, and look in dismay at my muddied hands and dusty skirts. There is no time to change. When Edmund ducks beneath the lintel of the gate, I am still untying the strings of my apron. His smile is broad, his clothes thick with the dust of the road.

"There you are, Margaret. I hope you are taking care of my son."

Jay bumbles forward to greet him, his tail like a banner in the wind, but Edmund keeps his eyes on me as he absentmindedly pats his dog's head. I cannot contain my smile as I shade my eyes from the sun, noticing how it glints on his hair, turning it into gold.

"I am indeed, my lord. Please, excuse the state of my clothes. I had not expected you this day."

He plucks a rose from a nearby bush and presents it to me, ignoring my mucky fingernails. Then he leads me round the garden, following the path beneath the arches of woodbine and wild briar.

"You have done well here. It is very pretty."

"Not just pretty, Edmund, it is beneficial too. Every plant grown here is a remedy or offers easement for some ailment or another."

Why can I not just take his praise as it is offered? Why must I defend my labours here? Is it so wrong to be considered trivial? "But you are right," I add as an afterthought. "As well as functional, it is also very pretty."

He has my hand tucked within his, held tight beneath his elbow. It is growing overwarm in his palm and I am tempted to withdraw it but I let it stay. He matches his step to mine as our walk continues.

"The child is well? He is growing?"

"Well, I am growing, my lord, so I presume your son is also."

Indeed, now the sickness is passing I am at last fattening like a goose for winter, and no longer resort to padding to achieve a womanly shape. I am still very short; my head doesn't even reach Edmund's shoulder. My brother-in-law, Jasper, often teases that I look more like Edmund's daughter than his wife. His jokes make my husband scowl; he never sees the humour in such jests. When we walk out in public, he urges me to wear heels or pattens to make me taller, and he scolds me for chewing my finger nails.

Edmund pauses and ushers me to the arbour, where we rest upon a seat of camomile. He fiddles with the ends of my girdle as he looks around the garden, his face anxious; regretful?

"What is it?" I ask, sensing he is concealing bad news. "Why are you looking like that?"

He pats my hand.

"Nothing to get alarmed about. It is just ... well, I am sorry, but you will have to leave this place after all your hard work."

"Leave?" I look around the garden in dismay. The plants standing shoulder to shoulder in the sun, the shrubs undulating in the light breeze, the insects busy in the blossoms. "And go where?"

"Lamphey. It will be easier there, a better base, and closer to Jasper at Pembroke."

"But you said we would be here until September. I had wished to reap the rewards of our labours. It would be easier for me to leave once the garden is readying for winter."

I bite my lip, regretting I will not see the garden come to full fruition. "Can I not stay here? I might be in your way at Lamphey."

He withdraws his hand.

"No. You are safer with me. I can keep a better watch on you there; if you should fall into enemy hands I dread to think ..."

"Of course I will come, Edmund," I say, seeking to hide my disappointment. "You are my husband, I am glad to do as you wish. I can always build another garden."

He turns toward me, his face full of pleasure.

"But you won't have to. I had quite forgotten. There is a fine garden at Lamphey already, one of the best stocked gardens I have ever seen; and a great library, stuffed with books. It is a lovely place, Margaret, fit for a countess, fit for a queen. Fit for you."

August 1456

Once more, my possessions are packed into boxes and loaded onto the back of a cart to be taken to the dock. Edmund says the journey will be quicker and easier by sea. I try not to remember the short voyage I took once with my mother, when we were battered and beleaguered by storms. On the day before we leave, I walk sorrowfully around the garden for one last time while Myfanwy plucks seed heads. She stows them in small labelled packets and tucks them in with her baggage.

"We can make another physic garden," she says with great determination. "There is always next year."

"Yes," I reply, but without much vigour. I am sad; tired of moving. I long to stay at Caldicot, and the journey to Lamphey holds no charm for me, but I allow myself to be bundled into a litter for the short ride to the dock.

I am jolted and bumped. It is too hot with the curtains closed, but when I ask for them to be drawn back, the sun burns me and I beg for them to be closed again. The road is dusty, there are too many flies, and every so often we pass a dead creature in the road and the cloying stench pervades my litter. I clamp a hand across my mouth and try to stifle the vomit that surges in my throat. Myfanwy sits opposite, clinging to the seat, her face green with the motion, tiny beads of perspiration anointing her brow.

"Edmund says it isn't far," I try to comfort her. She pulls a face.

"It has been too far already. We would have been better off riding."

"Edmund wouldn't hear of it."

"I swear if men had to travel in litters they would find a way to make it more comfortable."

I manage a laugh.

"Edmund said it was little more than a mile or so..."

"A mile? Surely we have travelled ten!"

The horses move downhill, and I cling to the side of the litter while we swing and jerk for the final part of the journey. At last someone calls a halt, the horses stop, and the world settles down again. We sit up. Myfanwy straightens her cap and veil, and pulls back the curtain. Edmund's face appears, red from the sun.

"All safe and sound?"

He extends a hand to help me alight and I grasp it gratefully, placing my feet on terra firma. Putting a hand to my back and squinting slightly in the bright sunshine, I look about.

A brisk wind buffets my face, tiny invigorating slaps of briny air that kiss my cheeks and stir my blood. My eye is drawn straight away to the fluttering pennants of a ship waiting at the dock, the deck swarming with men labouring our luggage aboard. Overhead, gulls are causing uproar; squawking, keening and turning in the sky. A sudden brisk breeze lifts a cloud of dust and tries to steal my veil, and I put up a hand to save it. I blink to clear dirt from my eye, turning blindly toward Jay's yelp. Through a blur of tears I see Ned urging the dog to leave the comfort of the produce cart in which he has travelled.

Ned tugs at the lead and the hound follows reluctantly, his bloodshot eye full of resentment. I dab my eyes. "Myfanwy." I point blindly in the direction of the litter. "I have left my psalter on the seat, can you fetch it please?"

The gang plank is springy beneath our feet and Edmund places a hand beneath my elbow to steady me. Men pause in their work to acknowledge our presence but Edmund dismisses them with a wave of his hand, urging them to continue with their task. He aids me as I step down onto the deck, and the surge of the sea makes my head swim, the sensation echoing deep within my gut.

"It will take a while to become accustomed to the motion," he says, his hand a steadying influence on my arm. As if to prove his words Myfanwy staggers toward us.

"Goodness," she whispers as she hands me my psalter. "We are not even under way yet and I feel as if I am in my cups."

Jay slumps at my husband's feet and prepares to sleep again.

"Don't get too comfortable, old fellow," Edmund laughs, nudging him with his toe. "Come, Margaret, let us settle you in your quarters. Maybe Jay can keep you company on the voyage."

Below deck it is dark and cool; a strange green light, a briny aroma, the ships timbers creaking like an ancient body kept too long from the fireside. To soften the harshness of life aboard, someone has heaped cushions and furs on the narrow bed. Betony is already busy, plumping the pillows, laying out a fresh robe and pouring cool water into a bowl.

Gratefully, I pull off my veil, and Myfanwy helps me remove my sleeves so I can wash away the megrims of the road. The ship rises with the swell of the tide and a cry comes from above, taken up by another; then a bell clangs, the timbers groan as the sails are unfurled and bellied by the wind. The ship lifts and dips again, and I know we are on our way.

In anticipation I sit on the bed and kick off my shoes, shake out my hair before stretching out on the covers. For a long time I watch the swaying lantern, trying to accustom myself to the sinking and rolling of the sea. It mesmerises me, my eyes grow heavy. I blink slowly ...

It is almost dark when I wake. Myfanwy is sprawled in sleep beside me, Jay at her feet. He doesn't so much as raise his head when I stumble from the bunk and tiptoe from the cabin to clamber up the ladder to the deck. The day is all but gone and, at first, I don't notice Edmund standing at the ship's rail, looking forward into the darkness as if to hasten our journey. I make my way toward him, still unsteady on my feet, and lurch suddenly against him as the ship tilts unexpectedly. I grab his sleeve and he turns, instinctively reaching out a protective hand to my shoulder.

"Margaret, you should have stayed below. Come, you will get chilled."

I think he means to send me to my cabin again, but instead he opens his cloak and beckons me into its warmth. I hesitate, unsure and shy of such intimacy. "Come," he says. "I will warm you."

I move closer and stand before him, looking out to sea with my back against his belly. He wraps us both in woolly warmth that smells faintly of horse and sweat. A fragrance that is strangely reassuring.

"I am surprised to find the night so chilly after such a hot day."

He rests his chin on my head, his voice rumbling in his chest as he replies.

"It is often so at sea, but at least our journey is short. You will soon be safe on shore and tucked up in bed at Lamphey."

When his hands slide down to caress the dome of my belly, my instinct is to draw away, but it is dark and no one can see, so I do not deter him. As if the child senses his father is close, he jerks suddenly, and Edmund pulls away in surprise.

"Was that ... ? Did he ... ?"

"Yes, my lord. That was your son. He is a rebellious fellow."

"Ha!" Edmund laughs aloud and replaces his hands, stroking and squeezing gently, encouraging the baby to move once more. When the child kicks again, Edmund is wildly excited. "He is lusty, and strong."

I murmur agreement, my head lolling back against his shoulder as he continues to engage with his unborn child. For a moment, I am happy, content with my lot and sure of the future.

"Tell me about Lamphey. Is it warm and free of damp? Is it a good place to bring forth a child?"

"I would not have brought you here if it wasn't. Lamphey is palatial. You know how bishops like their comfort. I have set aside chambers for your own personal use. They are close to mine, overlooking the gardens. I am certain you will find them to your liking."

"I am sure I will. What are your plans, Edmund? Will you stay close by?"

"It depends upon Gruffydd ap Nicholas and ... and the Herberts. I am ordered to bring him under control, to enforce the debts he owes the king and to take the castles he has in his possession. At least ... that *was* my order ..."

Sensing uncertainty, I turn in his arms and look up at his strong head silhouetted against the deep blue sky.

"What do you mean, my lord? What has happened?"

His hands find the swollen mound of my stomach again.

"I don't know for sure, but I sense all is not well. Jasper, when he returns, will have more news. Until then, I can only follow the orders of the king."

"He is ailing again, isn't he?"

"As I understand it."

"And York is in control. What will happen if ... if the king never returns to himself? The queen will want to rule until her son is of an age, yet I cannot imagine her working in conjunction with York, whom she hates so much."

"No."

"What about you, Edmund? You are the king's brother, couldn't you become her advisor?"

A bitter laugh rumbles in his chest.

"Take the place of your uncle Beaufort, you mean? I don't think so."

"But why?"

"Aghh." He lets go of my belly and pulls away from me. He runs his fingers through his hair, leaving it dishevelled, like a field of ripe corn scat asunder by a devilish wind. "I serve the king. I am not convinced that serving the queen would amount to the same thing. She is foreign; the people hate her and her policies are flawed. I do not believe you can quell the population with violence. If she is ever to make peace with York, she needs to appease him, not antagonise him and ... the queen is not the sort of woman who will ever do that."

A brief silence falls; he pulls me back against him, wraps me once more in his cloak, and rests his chin on my head. Rediscovering our former comfort, his hands slide again to my swollen womb.

"So you will side with York should he move against the queen?"

"No… Perhaps. Oh, I don't know. I must wait on my brother for news. For now, I must take one day at a time and follow the order I was given by the king when he was not in the thrall of madness."

Edmund is right; the journey by sea is quicker and more comfortable than rattling over land in a litter. We disembark at Tenby and take the high road along a ridge, through golden green countryside to Lamphey. Once more, Myfanwy and I are rattled in the litter, but just as I feel I can take no more, Edmund calls a halt.

A servant comes running with refreshment and soon I am cradling a cup of ale in my palms, looking across the soft rolling land that stretches to the sea. Behind me, the horses are stomping and steaming, tearing mouthfuls of grass, rolling it on their frothy tongues and chomping it between large yellow teeth. Myfanwy is some way apart. I can hear her berating Ned for some misdemeanour. When Edmund joins me, I smile, and let him refill my cup.

"If I drink much more, my lord, we will be forced to stop again before we are much farther along the road."

He smiles, flushes slightly, and pretends he is going to take my cup away. I draw it back. "I was jesting, my lord. I am as thirsty as a fish."

I dip my face into the cup; the ale is warm and refreshing.

"Not far to go now," he says. "I was wondering … if you would like to ride with me. You might be more comfortable than bouncing around in that."

He nods toward the litter, filling me with relief. Riding with him will mean close proximity, but I find this not so irksome now I am with child, for I know he will not follow me to my bed.

"It will indeed be more comfortable. Thank you, Edmund."

Shyly, I allow him to hoist me onto the saddle before him, and once I am settled, he urges the horse forward. After the confines of the litter, it is a joy to breathe in fresh air and look out across the landscape. In the distance, the sea twinkles, deep blue in the sunshine. I keep my eye on it, dazzled and calmed by its vast presence. When we reach the highest part of the ridgeway, Edmund reins in his horse.

"Look," he says, and I follow the line of his finger to where a high-walled palace slumbers in a wooded valley.

"Is that it? Is that Lamphey?"

"It is. What do you think?"

"It looks lovely from here."

"I am told it is one of the finest palaces in Wales, but I haven't visited them all."

The palace is the home of John de la Bere, the bishop of Wales, but he is presently at court, serving as the king's chaplain and has placed Lamphey at our disposal. The palace is larger than the castle at Caldicot, solid and welcoming, and I can tell I am going to like it. I shift a little on the pommel of Edmund's saddle. "It looks to be the perfect place to give birth to our son."

He squeezes his heels and as the horse walks on, Edmund's body moves lazily against mine, his arms a protective shield around me and the child I carry.

Jasper is expected very soon, and Myfanwy is trying, and failing, to conceal her excitement. He is expected to join us before supper, and all afternoon she has been trying on different gowns in readiness. She has exchanged one cap after another, changing her sleeves, asking if she looks better in green or yellow. I bend my head over my needlework and smile secretly.

"You look beautiful in anything, Myfanwy, and well you know it."

She pauses in her preening and peers into the looking glass, a hand to her unblemished cheek.

"Do you really think so, Margaret? Do you think Jasper would agree?"

"Well, he isn't blind, is he?" I reply waspishly. I shouldn't encourage her vanity, it is one of the cardinal sins but I can hardly deny it for truth is also a virtue. She smoothes down her skirts and twists and turns, trying to reassure herself that Jasper will agree.

Besides Myfanwy's gratification, much depends upon Jasper's visit and his news from court. Recent word from England informed us that the queen has moved the king's court to Kenilworth. The castle there is highly fortified, and against the wishes of York and his contingent, she is preparing to run the country herself.

Henry VI is now a puppet-king.

The crease on Edmund's brow deepens when he hears of it. He is curt with the servants and this morning he failed to pet Jay before riding out on the king's business.

I have discovered that if my husband is troubled, I am also. I may appear to be engrossed in the altar cloth I am stitching, but in reality, my mind is teeming with possible solutions. Of course, I am on the side of the king, the side of my husband, but my dilemma will be where to place my loyalty should Edmund fall foul of the queen. She is my mother's friend. I recall her brittle kindness toward me when I was a child; the king's simplistic doting. Henry is the rightful monarch, there is no doubt of that, but does she have the right to rule in his stead? I am not sure. There may be others who would serve the country better.

From her seat at the window, Myfanwy cries, "They are here." She leans out, her hair tumbling about her shoulders.

"Myfanwy, come away from there. Put your cap on."

I sound like an old maid, yet she is older by several years. She turns and pouts, but her eyes are glistening with impatience. I put down my sewing.

"I suppose you are right. It is time I made ready for the evening."

She jumps up and summons the maids to bring water, then rummages through my clothes press, drawing out my favourite kirtle and fresh linen for my approval. She then fidgets and fumes as I am made ready. Her excitement is slightly irritating. I have never enjoyed the feverish joys of a youthful amour and envy makes me mean. Just as we are about to leave I stop.

"Before we go, I must remember my devotions," I announce, and she watches in open-mouthed frustration while I kneel at my prie dieu, taking some delight in delaying, hoping it will teach her some patience.

When my knees begin to cramp, I rise slowly and she almost dances with delight when I signal for the door to be opened to facilitate our exit.

As soon as we enter the hall, Jasper and Edmund look up. My husband rises and Jasper swivels in his seat, watching as we cross the room; or rather, watching Myfanwy.

He barely notices me.

Both men welcome us to the table. Edmund's lips brush my cheek and Jasper bends over my hand, his eyes seeking out Myfanwy as soon as he straightens.

"My lady," he says. "You are radiant." I know his words are not for me. Myfanwy has flushed as rosy as a summer peach. We take our places at table and are not half way through the first course when the talk turns to the condition of the king.

"Even though the king has shown some signs of recovery, things are no better," Jasper says, prising a piece of meat from his teeth. "In fact, I'd say they are worse. York is resentful, the queen is demanding, and the king is weak – God's teeth, Edmund, even when he is in his right mind, he dithers. He can't make a decision and in the end comes down on the side of the queen, as if all he desires is a quiet life."

"And what of York, where is he?"

"He left court in a fit of temper. I'm not sure of his direction. It puts you in an uncomfortable position."

Edmund opens his eyes wide. "You are not wrong there, brother. If I take back the castles ap Nicholas has taken, I do so for the king, yet lately they were York's possessions. I am caught between the two."

"But surely, the castles were his only while he was Protector?"

I am so wrapped up in the conversation that I speak without thinking. The men turn to look at me and I turn pink with embarrassment. "I am sorry, my lord, do go on. I will not speak again."

"Margaret, you are right, of course." Jasper smiles at me quickly, slightly puzzled at my interruption. "Yet York is unlikely to see it that way. He sees himself as the protector of the realm whether we want and need him or not. As the official constable of the castles in question, York may well feel Edmund has stolen what is his and returned them to Henry."

"Yes, I see." I stumble over my words, his solicitous explanation making me feel more awkward than ever. Despite my status and condition, I am but a woman and my years mark me as a child. I bite my lip in an effort to prevent myself from speaking out of turn again.

Edmund takes a draught of ale while Jasper leans back, hooking an arm over the back of his chair.

"I have watchers at court, men who will bring me word the moment anything changes. Tomorrow, I must return to Pembroke, put a few things in order there."

"Is it far to Pembroke?" Myfanwy asks and, grateful that talk has turned to more general things, I turn with interest toward Jasper's reply.

"No; two or three miles or less. I go back to court in a day or so, but on my return, Edmund must find the time to bring you to visit. Pembroke is not as gracious as this. It is a fortress, not a palace."

"Lamphey is very beautiful," I say. "I am looking forward to tending the gardens and planting."

Jasper smiles in a bemused manner as if he cannot reconcile the idea of me quietly gardening in a palace filled with armoured men and my husband riding daily into danger. I subside into silence, smile ruefully at Myfanwy, who doesn't notice because she is gazing at Jasper.

I feel a niggle of impatience. He is just a man; a powerful and handsome one, but just a man nevertheless.

And she has no business mooning after someone of his status; no good will come of it. From the way he returns her warm looks I fear the attraction is returned but he can offer her nothing. And she certainly has nothing to offer him.

She is toying with her food, nibbling half-heartedly, but drinking freely of the wine. Now that the first sickly months of pregnancy have almost passed, I have discovered a new love of food. I partake of every course, and when a platter of honey-drenched wafers is placed before us, I eat Myfanwy's share as well as my own. Edmund watches with amusement, but like an indulgent parent, says nothing. When I am finished, he reaches across to wipe a trickle of honey from my chin. When he has done, he allows his hand to slide down my arm. He keeps me hand-fast for the rest of the meal.

The entertainers come on; first, a trio of minstrels who sing a mournful tune, lightened only by the antics of the tumblers who, too impatient to wait their turn, stage a hilarious re-enactment of the tragic tale. Jasper slams his cup onto the table, slopping wine and throws back his head, while my ladies titter behind their hands. I cannot help but join in the laughter, but feeling Edmund's eyes upon me, I turn to look at him. I sober suddenly when I catch him watching me; his eyes creased with … something I cannot identify.

In a day or two, he will be riding away. He will be gone for weeks, and I am surprised to discover I will miss him. I have grown used to him; he represents security, and warmth. I will miss our late night conversations in which we whisper of the future of our son, of the colour of his hair. We try to guess the hue of his eyes, and imagine his future position at the royal court.

When the revel ends, Edmund follows me to my chamber. He kicks off his boots and takes a seat close to the hearth. My women make themselves scarce and I follow them to the door, draw the bolts across and settle on the floor at my husband's feet. Jay lays his big head in my lap and Edmund pulls off my veil and begins to fiddle with my hair until I grow sleepy and my head lolls on his knee.

When the fire has reduced to embers, Edmund stirs. Reluctantly, for I hate him to treat me like a child, I allow him to put me to bed. He removes my pearl necklace and throws it on the dresser before fumbling with the laces of my gown. With a sound of triumph, it finally becomes free, and forms a blue-green pool at my feet. He kicks it away as if it is a rag and scoops me into his arms.

Once I am tucked beneath the covers, I lie on my side, snuggle into the mattress and prepare to drift off to sleep, conscious all the while of his stealthy movements as he removes his clothing.

The bed dips as he clambers in, his body a little chilled against mine. Once, I would have longed to move away, but now I am with child I sense no danger in his presence. He places his large hand on my hip, the warmth of his touch penetrating my thin shift. We are cupped together like spoons, his breath on my neck, his fingers gently kneading my waist. Something stirs within me, his child is nestling snug in my womb, and I relax against my husband as sleep drags me further into its embrace.

In my dream, someone is caressing me, slowly lifting my shift, cupping my belly, stroking, skimming my skin, filling me with warmth. I groan and stir, the caress ceases and, missing it, I groggily reach for the hand and replace it on my belly. Edmund emits a sigh and rolls me onto my back. I am half asleep, half awake, and do not remember to reject the softness of his lips upon my breast. I am flooded with warmth; a warmth that quite rapidly turns to heat, my body invaded by a sensation that is both alien and irresistible.

I am not Margaret. I have been consumed by some other being, some sensuous, erotic goddess who thrives beneath her husband's touch and urges him to continue. His mouth is on my breast, and his hands that skim my skin are my only reason for continuing to breathe. His own breath is coming in rasps, his hand travels down from my breast, burning a route across my belly before coming to rest between my legs, opening a path of pleasure as yet untrodden. I do not stop him. I have no wish to deter him, or to stay his hand. I don't want him to ever stop.

He is stirring places I did not know I had, giving me pleasure I had not known existed. I part my legs, press myself against him and wind my arms about his neck. His mouth comes down on mine, hard with longing, rough with desire, as his finger moves and my body shatters. Breath and life are suspended in one glorious moment, our cries mingling as his seed gushes wet upon my thigh.

Afterwards, we lie together, his forehead against mine as I try to peer through the darkness, the need to see his face overwhelming. For the first time I am not shamed. I feel blessed and newly alive.

Late August

The bailey is full of horses, carts and armoured men; the air alive with voices. Above the palace walls Edmund's flag snaps and bellies in the breeze. I stand on the steps of the hall, put on a brave face and wait to bid my husband goodbye.

Jay, who despite his age thinks his place is with his master, has hauled himself from his favourite haunt at the hearth and stands head down, waiting for someone to lift him onto a wagon. I put my hand on his head and he looks up at me, a sad question in his eyes.

"No, Jay. You are staying here with me. You are too old now to follow your master on the road."

Ned appears with a rope and loops it around the dog's collar. "Thank you, Ned," I murmur, noticing the resentment in his eye.

He is angry with me because I refused my permission for him to ride out with Edmund today. He complains that his place is on the road with the other men, not safe at home with the women and children. But I will not relent; I will not let him go. The wound left by the arrow has healed, but it has left him weak, his right arm devoid of muscle, and he still becomes breathless and remains very pale. He needs further nourishment and the ease of living in one place. I tell Edmund the boy will need another six months at least to regain his former vitality. Ned, when he discovers my order, is slow to forgive. I show my sympathy with a gentle smile but, grim-faced, he avoids my eye. I understand his resentment. It is just as I feel when I am forbidden to do something, so I do not reprimand him, but turn away. I am sure he will come to understand my reasons, but I know how hard it must be for him. It is hard for me, too, to be left behind.

Edmund's voice cuts through the babble. Flicking back my veil, I turn toward it. He is striding across the bailey in full armour with his gauntlets in hand. Beside him, his squire is hop-skipping along, carrying his helmet and sword. Edmund stops, takes my hand and draws me close, lowering his face to mine. As we kiss, a cheer goes up from the assembly and he pulls suddenly away, his face red. He gives a rueful smile before climbing onto his horse. It is a great beast, richly caparisoned, hooves striking sparks on the cobbles. Mounted, Edmund towers above me. I crane my neck, squinting into the sunshine before putting up a hand to shield my eyes.

"Good bye, Edmund." I try to speak confidently but my voice issues in a squeak of fear. "Be safe. I will pray for easy victory."

He grins and raises an arm, signalling for his men to follow, and nudges his horse on. As the household surges toward the gate and the dogs set up a great din of barking, the air around me fills with dust. Only Jay, Ned and I remain on the palace steps. For a long moment, we remain there. Unwilling to move, I feel strangely bereft; the diminishing noise of departure is somehow isolating and wretched.

Even when the women and children return to stand gossiping in the sunshine, I do not move. The sky is high above me, the ground solid beneath my feet. In my womb, Edmund's child squirms and kicks and, at my back, the Bishop's palace offers warmth and welcome, yet my equilibrium has shifted. I am thrown off balance.

I cannot settle to anything. My needlework lies abandoned on the table, my books open at the last page I read. Instead, I spend my days praying and nurturing my child. My knees grow raw from kneeling and a niggling pain in my lower back never lessens, even at night. From time to time, Edmund sends word, but his messages are sketchy, rushed notes, written in haste at the roadside. He does not say he is missing me, makes no mention of our new found affection, but he bids me care for my health and that of our son.

My days drag by. I pick up my needle again, reluctantly filling the empty space with tiny neat stitches. When I finally apply the last few strands of silk, I hold it aloft, satisfied to have conquered my idleness. I stare at the tiny loops and swirls of the pattern and remember stitching them, embroidering a life for myself, a future for my son. Myfanwy and I carry it carefully to Lamphey's tiny chapel and drape it across the altar, where I pray thrice daily and sometimes during the lonely, chilly nights.

As the end of August nears, I begin to work on garments for the baby. The cap in my hand is so tiny, I cannot imagine a head small enough to fit it, yet my women assure me it will be so. As my needle dips in and out of a sea of white linen, I dream of Edmund's victorious return, his joy at the arrival of his son. I picture our heads close together, watching as the baby sleeps in his wooden crib, but as the weeks pass and my worries increase, I begin to wonder if that dream will ever become real. I withdraw from everyone. Whenever I can, I sneak off on my own, wishing only to be alone with God and my child, my son whom Edmund says we must name Owain.

I am in the garden, tucked out of sight in an arbour, sewing as usual, when Ned appears. I am unaware of his presence until I hear his shy cough. I look up.

"Ned! You startled me." I lower my needle and wait for him to speak. He is grinning from ear to ear so I know the news is good. "Is there a message from my husband?" I prompt.

"Not a message by his hand, my lady, but a tinker came by bearing news from Carmarthen."

"Yes, go on, tell me."

"Our lord has taken the castle, my lady. The Welshman has fled and the earl now turns his attention to Cydweli, and Aberystwyth."

"That is good news." I turn the full force of my pleasure on him, making him blush to the roots of his hair. He opens his mouth to speak but a footstep on the path forestalls him.

"Myfanwy, did you hear the news?"

"I did. I had come to tell you of it but I see Ned got to you first."

At my invitation, she joins me on the chamomile seat and bends over to examine my needlework. Hopefully, I tell myself, in a few weeks we can join Edmund at one of the castles he has secured for the king. Although Lamphey is tranquil and a good place to be nurturing a child, I will feel safer closer to my husband.

October 1456

Time seems to stop; the hours and days become weeks and years. My life is in limbo, I am in a palace not my own, waiting for my husband, waiting for my child to be born. My duties are those of a matron, and as my belly stretches, I forget I am just thirteen years old. I feel old, as if I have experienced all there is. I scratch beneath Jay's ears, teasing out the burrs in his coat with a comb, and remember when I used to run through the meadows at Bletsoe with my siblings. It seems so long ago. I wish I could laugh and run now.

The summer is almost over, the garden going to seed, the still-room well stocked with remedies and salves. The world around me is preparing to shut down for winter, and it won't be long before my child arrives. I run a hand across the tight bowl of my belly and wonder what Edmund will think when he is reunited with his apple-shaped wife.

At last, he has agreed to let me join him in Carmarthen and I must leave this place. Although I have come to love Lamphey, I am not sorry; my place is with Edmund. Slowly, as my belongings are packed into boxes, the room grows bare around me until just Jay and I are left at the hearth. Tomorrow morning we will ride away from Lamphey, but I intend to return. I love the palace and the gardens, and will miss the rich treasures stored upon the library shelves. When Edmund has restored peace in the land, I tell myself we will come here again and let our children run wild in the gardens.

I cast a lingering look about the empty chamber and wonder where Myfanwy is. She is probably ensuring my jewels and gowns are laid away with great care. She will be ordering the servants, attempting to organise the other women, who resent her lowly status. I sigh a little, feeling lonely, wishing she were with me.

The months ahead are full of the unknown. I am very young to birth a child; there are those who frown upon Edmund for not waiting until I was older, but I understand his reasons. Once I have presented him with his child, many assets will be bestowed upon Edmund, strengthening both our bond and our child's future. I know how important a son is to him; it is important to me, too. But that does not stop me from being afraid.

God will keep you safe, I tell myself, and I try very hard to believe it but I am growing maudlin. At my feet, Jay yawns and drops his head onto his paws as if he is dismal too. In the empty room, I blink away tears, bend my head over my sewing again and listen to the crackling fire in the grate.

In the morning a gentle rain is falling; the sort that is much akin to mist but that wets you right through to the skin until it seems to seep into your very soul. We are all in bleak spirits and I am loath to leave the comfort of the palace. Myfanwy and I climb into the litter and order the curtains drawn. The horses put their heads down; the armed guard pull their collars high and their helmets low.

Ned is fortunate, his role as Jay's companion gaining him a place in the covered produce cart. The journey is a jolting one. The road is quickly mired, and more than once we are forced to stop because a wagon has come to grief. For once, I am grateful for my dry, snug litter.

While those on horseback are quickly wet through, I am seated upon soft cushions, with a rug for my knees. At first, Myfanwy entertains me with her chatter; she is excited to be on the road, and keeps peeping from beneath the curtain.

"I can hardly see across the valley," she says, letting the drape fall. "I hope we will reach shelter before dark."

"Of course we will." I don't mean to snap but her words fill me with fear. The thought of being out on the road after darkness has fallen is unthinkable. "There must be a monastic house along the route; perhaps we should give orders to make an early stop."

She subsides into silence. I read, doze off to sleep, but awaken suddenly at an extra violent jolt of the litter. For what seems like hours, we lumber slowly across the countryside. As the horses begin to move downhill, the swaying of the litter increases, the book I've been reading slides to the floor and I cling to my seat. When the terrain levels out and the motion becomes a little less sickening, Myfanwy picks up my book.

"Thank you ..." Further conversation is stolen by the sound of a galloping horse. I throw up the curtain and poke out my head, blinking into the rain that settles on my cheeks like a diaphanous mask.

"What is it?"

A young page is shouting, gesturing wildly, pointing back the way we've come. My steward leaps from his horse and splashes toward me.

"Bad tidings from your husband, my lady. William Herbert and the Vaughans have attacked Carmarthen. My instructions are to take you back to Lamphey."

I fall back on my pillows.

"But we have come so far," I wail. Myfanwy joins me on my seat, offers me a kerchief to soak up my ready tears.

The men refuse to heed my arguments. Edmund's orders are written large; they wave his heavy black scrawl beneath my nose and stand firm against my pleading. Knowing I am beaten, I scribble a hasty message to Edmund, requesting that he send me word as soon as he is safe. Sealing the letter with a prayer and a secret kiss, I hand it to the boy, watch him mount his sweating horse and ride away into the mist.

Aware of possible danger, we travel more quickly now, all thought of my delicate condition forgotten. Desolation swamps me as the litter sways and rattles back the way we have come. Even when the rain ceases and the sun pokes blearily from behind the clouds, I cannot raise a smile. I cannot even pretend optimism. Myfanwy does her best to comfort me, but I turn a little away from her and bury myself in my own thoughts until she subsides.

We have travelled but three miles when a shout goes up behind and the messenger returns. He slides from his horse, his chest heaving, his hair plastered to his head.

"I could not get through," he shouts through the increasing rain. "There are soldiers on the road, and the castle is surrounded."

The steward frowns, glances up as the rain begins to come down harder, spattering noisily through the leaves overhead. "We must move more quickly, my lady; we must get you to safety. Will you ride with me?"

I hesitate, my eyes swivelling from Myfanwy's pallor to his darkly serious face. Such a thing is highly irregular.

"We could go to Pembroke," Myfanwy says suddenly, breaking her silence. "You would be under the protection of Jasper then."

Her face is anxious, insistent. I narrow my eyes, angered at her blatant romantic strategy in our time of danger.

"Jasper is at court. And you should address him as Lord Pembroke."

She turns away, pouting.

Myfanwy and I both know how vulnerable we are. Despite my status and our heavily armed guard, we are a target for the desperate, and a rich prize for my husband's enemies. My belly is tight and hard, the child quiet and heavy within me. My stomach churns at the danger I have placed him in and I suppress a sob, wishing I had never left the safety of Lamphey palace. I am at a loss as to what to do. The steward shuffles impatiently.

"There is an abbey not far from here, a Cistercian brotherhood, where we could seek shelter."

Ned, his hand to Jay's collar, watches me with round, anxious eyes, waiting for my answer. Suddenly I realise it is not just my own safety I must look to; our entire party are in peril. I nod my head once in agreement, both embarrassed and afraid.

As I am hauled inelegantly up before the steward I manage to send the boy a rueful smile. Summoning what dignity I can, I settle on the pommel and the steward apologises as he puts his arms around me, holding me secure, guarding me with his body. He gathers up the reins, jabs the horse with his heels and we jerk forward, mud splashing all around us.

It is very strange to be in such close proximity with a man who is not my husband, but I am grateful for the protection and the warmth of the steward's body. I put my head down and close my eyes against the driving rain. With stone-cold fingers, I cling to the horse's mane, and try not to think of the earth speeding past beneath me. I try not to think of my unborn child, who lies as quiet as a boulder in my tight belly.

Every mile we travel takes me farther from Edmund. I try to remember his face, cling to our shared vision of the life we will lead when the fighting is over and our child is born.

Yet all around me the world is bleak, the landscape obliterated by driving rain, my husband in absolute peril, and myself and my child at God's mercy. I try but fail to muster the picture of domesticity I hope will come after.

Whitland Abbey – November 1456

Safe in the confines of Whitland Abbey, I huddle close to the fire, unable to prevent the juddering of my frozen, frightened body. As soon as my blood is warm enough to allow my fingers to work, I summon a pen and parchment. With no recourse to etiquette, I scribble an urgent message to Jasper who is with the king at Kenilworth.

I wish with all my heart he was here in Wales. Were he at Pembroke he could be here before dusk but it could be many days before my message reaches him and he rides to relieve his brother. I am confused. Why has Edmund come under attack? He is following the orders of his king, why does York send an army against him?

When he comes to enquire as to my comfort, I bombard the steward with questions.

"York is jealous of your husband's position. He fears his kinship with the king will interfere with his own plans. He sees Carmarthen and the other Welsh castles the earl has taken as his own by right, and he has stepped so far from royal favour he probably believes his position is lost."

Unable to mask my confusion I look up at him.

"I wonder what he will do next." I keep my voice low; afraid to speak too loudly in case it gives my fears substance. I look about the stark room that remains stubbornly chilly in spite of the lively fire, and wish I had never left the warmth and comfort of Lamphey Palace. "Do you think he will hurt Edmund? He is the king's own brother. Surely even York would not go so far."

My voice shakes, my chin trembles. I clench my lips in an effort to still my tears. I must remember my position. I am not some silly little girl. I am the Countess of Richmond.

After the messenger has ridden away I cannot seem to either keep still or warm myself so I wrap my cloak tight about my body and pace back and forth from one side of the chamber to the other. Every so often, I stop to stand on tip-toe and peer from the narrow window, but there is nothing to see; just a bleak, cold vista and relentless, lashing rain.

I think of Edmund. I wonder where he is, what he is doing. He could be fighting; he could, even now, be victorious. Or he could be captured or wounded. He could be *dead*.

I turn too quickly on my heel and the room sways and dips around me. My hand snakes out, finds solidity, and I discover Myfanwy has come to stand beside me. I welcome her substance and grip her arm, the warmth of her flesh a sharp contrast to my frozen fingers.

"Come along, my lady. You must stop this or you will make yourself ill. Think of your child."

Our faces are close together. I can see the pores of her skin, the sheen of perspiration on her brow. Her eyes are creased with concern, shadowed with worry.

"How can I rest when Edmund is in danger? How can I think of anything else?"

"Now, now, my lady; your husband would want you to think only of yourself and his son at this time. You must stay strong so you are able to greet him happily on his return."

I sigh and let my head droop on her shoulder.

"Oh, Myfanwy, I am so afraid."

"Of course you are; who would not be? But you have a duty both as wife and mother, and your duty is to put your health first. Edmund is a fine soldier and big enough to look to himself."

She is right. Wearily, I allow her to lead me to the bed where she begins to unlace my gown. When I am tucked beneath the blankets, she brushes my hair from my brow as my nurse used to when I was an infant, and a sudden memory of the nursery washes over me. A tear trickles from the corner of my eye, quickly pursued by another.

"I had not realised you cared for him so much," she whispers, her eyes searching mine. I feel a blush creeping up my neck and blooming on my cheeks.

"Neither had I," I murmur.

***

For three days, I am in limbo, voluntarily imprisoned in the abbey while we await news. Stealthily we send messengers to discover news, but it is almost the end of the third day before a message finally arrives. I snatch it from the boy's hand, tear it apart and drink in the words that confirm my worst fears. Edmund has been taken and is imprisoned in Carmarthen castle. My hand shakes as I scan the words again. The letter is in a strange hand but at the bottom my husband has scrawled a few words that give me a little hope.

I am injured but well. Take care of our son. I will be with you soon.

I drink in the information, read it over again and again before I begin to believe it.

"At least he is alive," I manage to utter as the letter falls from my fingers to lie among the rushes. My heart floods with thankfulness.

After summoning Myfanwy, we hurry to the church where I pour out my gratitude to God for sparing him. All we need to do now is persuade York to set him free. Edmund must be forced to come to any terms demanded to ensure his release. His freedom is what matters most. After forcing myself to eat the meagre supper provided, I call for the steward and together we fashion a message to begin the negotiations for his release.

When we learn that York and his followers have left Carmarthen and turned their attention to Aberystwyth, I grow impatient. The need for caution has passed. I want to ride for Carmarthen straight away, to ascertain that he is unharmed, but Myfanwy's wisdom hinders me.

"Please, wait for Jasper," she implores. "He cannot be long away and we will be safe with him. When he gets here, with the men of Pembroke behind him, he will put pressure on York to free Edmund and bring him home to you. It would be far better if we were to return to Lamphey and wait for him there."

"No; not without Edmund. It is almost November. I will wait three more days for Jasper, if he is not here by then I will ride to Carmarthen ... alone if I have to."

***

Another long road. Another jolting, disheartening journey in the litter. Try as I might to persuade him, Jasper is unbending.

"You will ride in the litter or not at all," he says, attempting to soften his harsh words with a quick smile. Pouting like an unruly child, I gather my cloak about me and clamber into the detested conveyance. I sit bolt upright, simmering with anger for as long as I can bear to. Myfanwy, moonstruck by Jasper's return, smiles an apology for my behaviour and tries to soothe me.

"The journey will not be so long this time," she says, "and Jasper is only thinking of your safety, and that of the babe." She nods toward the dome of my belly and instinctively I put a hand on it, the contact imperceptibly softening my mood.

"I know." Full of resentment, I look out beyond the looped-back curtain. Mercifully the weather is dry; a chilly bright day, with the sun reflecting on the puddles left by the last few weeks of rain. The blue skies are a teasing reminder of the summer so recently departed. Tomorrow, it will rain again.

Jasper rides at the head of the column. I watch his upright figure, notice how his head continually moves from left to right as he scans the horizon for signs of trouble. He is uneasy, not convinced of York's promise of safe passage, and his discomfort unnerves me too.

Where the terrain allows, we follow the serpentine trail of the River Tywi, but every so often, to avoid marshy terrain, we are forced to higher ground. As we pass close to Grey Friars, the waterlogged fields about the river are scattered with sheep. At our approach, they throw up their heads in alarm and abandon their grazing to hurry from our path. Myfanwy laughs.

"Look at them. They look like beggars with their grubby woollen fleeces hanging from their backs."

I smile, but I do not care about sheep. In the distance, I have spied the town gate and beyond it the towers of Carmarthen Castle standing proudly above a loop at the river crossing.

I sit up straighter and try to see ahead, as if expecting Edmund to be waving a greeting from the battlement. But he does not know I am coming; I will be the last person he expects to see.

I watch Jasper ride toward the town gate. He leans from his saddle and exchanges words with the gatekeeper. He takes off his helmet and turns toward me, the wind tussling his hair which, I notice with a sudden pang, is the exact same shade as Edmund's. His brow is creased and, noting his dour expression, I sense more trouble. My heart sinks as, after a further exchange of words, he turns his horse and rides back to the litter.

He slides from his horse.

"Margaret ..." He hesitates, pulls a face and lets out a long breath. "There is pestilence here. I cannot let you travel farther. It isn't safe."

A surge of anger such as I have never known consumes me; I can feel it rushing uncontrollably through my body, gathering in my head until I feel it will burst.

"I will not be kept from him!" I hear myself shout. Tears of rage drench my cheeks; my fists are clenched tight, my ears ringing with the sudden stress. My mother would be furious if she witnessed such behaviour, but I am too afraid and too angry to care. Without ceasing my tirade, I swing my legs toward the door.

"I have travelled too far and waited too long to be kept away now. If there is pestilence here, he may need nursing. I will not allow you to keep me from my duty."

I struggle from the litter and, shrugging Myfanwy's hand from my shoulder, begin to hurry along the dirt track, determined to travel the rest of the way on foot. I do not get far before my ankle turns on a rut in the road. Concealing the sudden sharp pain, I limp on.

"Margaret!" Jasper, defying all etiquette, strides after me, grabs my arm and forces me to stop. "You are acting like a child. Get back in the litter. I will take you as far as Grey Friars, but there you must wait until I discover the situation at the castle. If it is safe, you can see Edmund tomorrow. For Christ's sake, think of your son."

I am always being told to think of my child. I think of little else. I am thinking of him now, in my desperation to liberate Edmund. What will my son be without his father?

Myfanwy adds her argument to Jasper's, her voice soft and silky with persuasion.

"We can freshen up and rest at the priory. You will feel better tomorrow, my lady, after a night's sleep. Edmund will prefer to see you calm and ... clean." She casts a glance at my mired skirts.

I pass a hand over my face, knowing I am beaten, knowing they are right. With a sob of both rage and misery, I allow myself to be turned around and bundled back into the hateful litter.

As the horses lurch forward and the swaying of the litter starts up again, I refuse to look at Myfanwy. I resent her alliance with Jasper. Despite my situation, I do not miss the warm looks that pass between them, or the excuses she finds to be with him. She is glad this mischance has befallen my husband because it puts her in the company of her sweetheart.

Another religious house, this time run by the Grey Friars. They greet me cordially, offer what comfort they can and give me lodging in the abbot's house. The room is comfortable, well furnished, and a welcome fire roars in the grate. Fuelled with resentment toward her, I cruelly send Myfanwy from my presence. It is midnight before I regret it. I pass a lonely, miserable night but I am too stubborn to summon her back, and so I lie awake, staring into the dark.

The child is quiet, his head pressing on my bladder, so I have to get up repeatedly to use the close-stool. Each time I return to the bed, the sheets become rucked into a worse mess and by dawn the blankets look as though a wrestling match has taken place.

"Goodness," Myfanwy exclaims in the morning when she brings me a tray of victuals to break my fast. "What have you been doing?"

She bears no malice for my hostility the night before and her cheeks are rosy, her eyes bright as if she has passed a restful night. While I stare grumpily at my morning meal, she begins to smooth the sheet and plump my pillows.

"Jasper will be leaving soon, I expect." She moves to the window and opens the shutters, letting a stream of dirty daylight into the room.

I want to correct her, command her to use his proper title but I am tired, sick and tired of everything and cannot find the strength. I frown at the hump of my raised knees beneath the blanket. There must be something I can do, some action I can take.

I push away the tray and throw off the covers. "Help me get dressed, Myfanwy. I cannot face food this morning."

Cup in hand, she hovers for a few moments before hurrying to do my bidding. I am mute during my toilette, but all the while she sponges my face her questions fall as swiftly as arrows.

"Why are you in such a hurry? What are you going to do? You don't mean to defy Jasper, do you, Margaret? Please don't do anything ..."

"Give me that." I snatch the comb rudely from her hand and begin to drag it through my hair. It catches at the knots, large clumps coming free. "There," I say. "Now quickly braid it and tuck it under my cap."

She has no option but to obey me, and I offer no explanation. Ten minutes later, less neat than usual, I am waiting for Jasper to appear in the hall. I hear his approach long before he arrives.

"Margaret." He stops short, instantly wary as he notices my outdoor clothes and my mulish expression. He tucks his helmet defensively beneath his arm. "What are you doing here?"

I can tell by his voice that he knows my intention, but I raise my chin defiantly before I make an answer.

"I am coming with you. I will not be sent to my chambers like a child. My husband's life may be in peril and I refuse to sit idly by when it is clearly my duty to be with him."

"It is too dangerous." He comes closer, his brow creased with concern. "I have no idea what danger we may be riding into. Do you not care about your child or your own well-being?"

"Of course I do." I look him firmly in the eye. "I have spent most of the night in prayer asking for God's guidance as to what I should do. He convinces me my place is at Edmund's side. Surely, Jasper, you are not so high and mighty as to argue with God?"

Exasperated, he looks at the ceiling, and then back at me.

"By Heaven, Margaret, you could use a spanking."

I stiffen, outraged at his discourtesy, but as I open my mouth to make a sharp retort, I think I detect a tiny spark of admiration in his eye. I close my mouth again and make no reply as I pull on my gauntlets.

"And I am not spending another moment in that litter. Have a horse made ready for me." I speak over his shoulder to his steward, but Jasper puts up a hand.

"No, if I have any say in the matter, you will ride with me, my lady, so I can at least try to keep you from harm."

As he ushers me from the room Ned steps forward, seemingly from nowhere. "My lady, I am coming too."

A sigh shudders from deep within me. I do not even turn to look him in the eye.

"Don't be tiresome, Ned. Go and walk Jay in the gardens, make yourself useful."

I turn again but he tags after me.

"Begging your pardon, my lady, but I owe you my life, and if you are going into danger then I am coming with you." He puts his hand on the dog's head. "And so is Jay."

"Oh, for Heaven's sake, you impossible child. Very well, do as you wish. I revoke all responsibility for you."

There is no time to argue. I march swiftly away, Jasper at my side telling me I am too soft with the boy. I raise my eyebrows but forebear to comment that he might likewise be too soft with me.

***

I have never seen suffering or poverty before, but perhaps I have never looked. The streets of Carmarthen are squalid; there are dead dogs in the gutter, heaps of refuse at the roadside. Beggars sit in the dirt, dogs and rats scavenge in the gutters. I see ragged people, blind men, children with ribs like hoops, women little older than I already worn to the bone by hunger. And now, to add to their misery, pestilence has visited Carmarthen.

As if seeing the scene from above, I am aware of the bright opulent splash of our party against the sombre backdrop of the town. Above our heads, Jasper's pennant flaps and snaps in the breeze, the sun glinting on the armour of the guard. The people at the roadside sullenly watch us pass, as different to us as the moon is from the sun. I am warm in my plush velvet gown, my pristine linen and my thick fur cloak. Cradled in Jasper's arms, kept safe by the host of men at arms that surround us, I know myself for a pampered, fortunate soul, and for the first time, I am shamed by it.

"Jasper, have you any coin about you? Can we give them some?"

"No." His voice rumbles in his chest as he rides on, his eyes fixed on the road ahead. "It would cause a riot. If you want to help them, give money to the friars, they in turn will help the needy."

I decide to do just that. I will ensure an annual sum is sent to the people here at Carmarthen. No creature living should have to suffer such penury.

The horses begin the steep climb to the castle where the shelters gradually grow less squalid and the peasants are marginally better dressed. As the shadow of the castle engulfs us, I suppress a shiver, starting in fear when a sudden cry goes up from the battlement. The gatekeeper peers out through a slit in the door. "Who goes there?"

"Open up for the Earl of Pembroke," Jasper growls. There is a scuffle within, but we are forced to wait for what seems a long time. At first I think we are to be ignored but eventually we hear the clanking chain as the portcullis slowly rises. I crane my neck, blinking against the bright sky, hoping to see Edmund leaning over the battlement, waving in greeting. But the parapet is empty.

The castellan wipes away the sweat on his brow with his sleeve. "I'm warnin' ye', there's pestilence within." He leers at me as Jasper urges our mount through the yawning gate. We move forward to the sound of hooves as our company clatters over the drawbridge. Jasper puts pressure on the reins, leaning back in the saddle, and we come to a halt in the middle of the bailey.

There is as much chaos here as outside. The inner ward is littered with bodies of both the sick and the dead.

I have a sudden longing for the gardens at Lamphey and Caldicot. Jasper's arms tighten around me.

"By Christ, Margaret, I should never have brought you here."

Ignoring him I lean forward and call out to the castellan who has shuffled in our wake. "The Earl of Richmond, where is he lodged?"

He spits on the ground and waves his arm in the direction of the western tower. I wriggle desperately, demanding to be let down from the horse. Jasper releases me reluctantly, swings from the saddle and helps me alight. With a fearful glance around the bailey, I slip my hand in his, and, picking our way through prone bodies, we hurry in search of my husband.

The steps to the upper chambers of the tower are narrow and winding, the torches almost burned out, some of them guttering to darkness as we pass. The air I breathe is dank as I feel my way in the gloom, the wall cold and weeping beneath my fingers. Behind me, I can hear Jasper's heavy tread, his rapid breathing, and I sense he is as anxious as I. Still, I am comforted to have him there.

Near the top, I pause for breath before pushing open a door. It creaks loudly, releasing a sweet cloying stench of mortal sickness. As horror washes over me, I whisper a desperate prayer, clamp a kerchief to my nose, and step into the chamber with Jasper close behind me.

His hand falls heavily upon my shoulder, our footsteps moving in unison as we draw toward the centre of the room. The shutters are half-closed, the fire dwindling. In the corner, on a narrow bed, I can just discern the figure of a man. He is thrashing and whimpering, caught in the agonies of a seizure. Shaking off Jasper's restraint, I hurry forward and sink to my knees at the side of the bed.

"Edmund." Although he gives no sign of recognition, he clutches my hand as if his life depends on it. I am a shaky lifeline indeed. My first instinct is to collapse, rely on the man behind me but the suffering on my husband's face makes that impossible.

I brush away the tears, turn my head and yell over my shoulder. "Get help, bring water, and send to the Grey Friars for Myfanwy. Tell her to bring medicine. Quickly!"

I barely acknowledge the sound of scampering feet as my order is obeyed. I look about me. What can I do? I am helpless. Why am I such a fool? Why did I not think to bring my remedies from the still-room? There are no herbs powerful enough to cure the plague, but there are some that provide relief.

"Edmund." I call to him again, reaching out to stroke back his damp and dirty hair. I hold his head still, my thumbs tracing the outline of his brow. "I am here now, all will be well, my husband."

He does not know me. His jaw is clenched as he shakes and shivers, his long legs juddering beneath a meagre blanket. I draw it back and notice his torso is swathed in a dirty bandage, stained by an oozing wound in his side. I remember the words from his message: *I am injured but well.*

He lied in his letter. For my sake he had made light of his injuries, but together with the plague, he has little hope now. I push away the thought, steel my strength and refuse to give in to the fear. I must do everything I can.

An hour later, Edmund is calmer but still unconscious. I have bathed him with tepid water, removed his linen and wrapped him in a fresh, clean sheet. His sweat-darkened hair is brushed away from a face that gleams bone-white in the gloom.

Jasper brings me a stool and I remember to reward him with a grateful smile.

"We should leave now, Margaret. You need to cleanse yourself, burn all your clothing, lest you too succumb."

I shake my head. "I don't believe he has much longer. I will stay with him until he departs."

I feel no panic now, the hysteria has vanished. I sit passively at his side and pray for an easy passing. As his hand grows limp in mine, I try not to dwell on our precious dreams that are dying with him.

I do not think of the past, or the wrongs he has done me. I have forgotten the monster my childish mind envisaged before we wed. He was … is … a man like many others; an ambitious man whose chief concerns are family and power, and fortune. If only the love between us had blossomed sooner; if only our son had been conceived with love. Edmund would have made a good father, a good husband, and I am grieved that our time together has been cut so short.

With little hope, I bow my head and pray again, trying to force God to listen to my will. But miracles do not happen any more so I do not ask that his life be spared. I ask only for a swift and painless passing.

Silently, in the corner, Myfanwy clutches a bundle of bandages in her arms and waits and watches, her face a white, open question. With tears on his cheek, Ned kneels at her feet, nervous, frantic fingers working in Jay's brindle fur. Jasper's hand is gentle on my shoulder, the pressure comforting in the darkness that is consuming my world.

As we sit there, suspended in time, Jay pulls free of Ned's grasp and comes to join me at the bedside. He settles on his haunches and, as Edmund's soul passes, he lifts his nose to the heavens and howls his sorrow.

We all feel like howling.

Grey Friars, Carmarthen – November 1456

I know nothing of the journey back to the priory. I come back to my senses some time later, and as if by sorcery, I find myself there. Silently, Myfanwy strips away my soiled clothing. She sends everyone away, and then takes everything, even my small linen. I watch as she struggles from her own garments, gathers up the bundle and summons Ned, ordering him to see that it is all burned. "And do the same with your own clothes," she calls after him.

"What are you doing?"

She glances up, the bones of her face hard.

"I don't know. When I was a child and there was pestilence in the village, a wise woman there insisted that we do the same. I have little hope that such measures will be effective."

I tremble, lost in stunned silence as she wraps me in a clean sheet and tells me to wait while a wooden tub is filled with water. There is no time for sweet-scented petals or delicate oils. In a miserable daze, I lower myself into the water and allow her to scrub me, head to toe, with soap so harsh it makes my eyes sting. Then, after roughly drying me and settling me before the fire, she immerses herself in the water too. I watch her scrub every inch of her smooth sleek body. She stands, the water cascading from her flanks and dripping from her long wet hair. Catching up a towel she wraps herself up and comes to me, kneels at my feet, takes both hands.

"Are you dry, my lady? Let me dress you."

I stand up and the sheet falls away. I cross myself, one arm over my hard pink breasts and the other to cradle my swollen belly. She quickly brings a loose gown and swamps me in fur and velvet, leads me to the bed. I follow her like a child and let her tuck me between the sheets. Yet the bed offers no comfort.

I roll onto my side and stare at the damp spots on the wall. I do not notice when my eyes grow heavy but it must be hours later that I wake to the sound of voices. Keeping my eyes closed, I listen as they plan my future.

"We must get her back to Lamphey..." Myfanwy whispers, but her words are cut short by Jasper's voice, that rasping deep and worried in the dark.

"Nay, not Lamphey. I have no jurisdiction there. I will take her to Pembroke. It is no palace, and the lodgings are not what she is used to, but it is safe ... impenetrable. She can bring forth her child in safety there."

"I must stay with her."

"I know. We both have need of you ..." His voice is cut short and a long silence follows, and then a scuffle in the shadows, a gentle moan. Stretching my legs to the end of the bed, I roll over onto my back. Instantly Myfanwy is beside me.

She lights a candle and I see her cap is gone. Her hair is awry and a strange expression gleams in her eye, as if she is lit up from the inside.

"You're awake, my lady. Can I get you anything? Look, your brother-in-law has called to see how you are."

I pull myself up on the pillows, place my hands on my belly and watch Myfanwy fussing around as she prepares a cup of wine.

Jasper comes to the foot of the bed. His face is pale and he is shadowed about the eyes. I remember he shares my loss, and I flinch as a vision of Edmund lying stiff and cold in his winding sheet rises before my eyes. Grief and fear swamp me again.

I turn my face away.

Jasper waves a hand around the room. "We must get you away from here, Margaret. The pestilence is spreading. I am taking you to Pembroke in the morning. You will be safe there."

I have no will to travel further. I would gladly stay here and die among the Grey Friars, but I have no strength for argument.

Indeed, it matters little to me where I am.

The Dowager Countess

Pembroke Castle stands impregnable on a crag above a loop in the river. Although Jasper warned me to expect a grim, grey, uncompromising stronghold, I am ill-prepared for it. The fortress offers no prospect of ease. The horses strain up the hill, the swaying and jerking of the litter adding to my misery and discomfort. I send up thanks to God that my journeying will soon be at an end.

As we approach the great gate, a shout goes up, echoed by another and another until, slowly, the drawbridge begins to lower and the portcullis is raised, giving vent to the life and noise within. With a jolt, the horses move on and we pass into the shadow of the gatehouse. For a moment the sun is extinguished and the chill increases, but when we emerge the other side, the sun returns in blinding glory.

I blink in the sudden light as Ned helps me clamber in an ungainly manner from the litter. Stretching my aching limbs, I look about the outer ward. It is heaving with activity; a boy with a stick drives a flock of geese by, pigs are squealing in a muddy enclosure, and the air is filled with the sharp acrid smell of a forge, where a blacksmith pauses in his work. Hammer in hand, he draws his forearm across his forehead, our eyes catch and he pulls off his cap in greeting. I do not smile in return but turn my face toward the aroma of roasting pig coming from the kitchens. The smell teases my reluctant taste buds back to life.

The people here have been expecting me, everyone pauses in their tasks for the first taste of the pregnant widow-child so suddenly in their midst. I do not acknowledge them. My eyes travel about my new home, my head rolling back so I can look upward, where the crenellations bite the sky and Jasper's flag hangs limp, as if in sorrow.

My host appears at my side, looking pale and uncomfortable beneath the dust of the road.

"My lady, come with me. I am ill-prepared for you, especially … like this … in your condit …" His words tail off hopelessly, and in an attempt to comfort him, I manage a rictus smile.

"I will be safe here, my lord. That is all that matters. As long as I have a roof over my head, and a fire in the hearth, I will be well."

Relief swamps his face, and a smile vanishes before it is truly formed. "We may even find you a straw mattress and a blanket," he quips. "No, truly, Margaret, Pembroke may lack the niceties to which you are accustomed, but we will do our best."

He ushers me up a sweep of stone stairs and I duck my head beneath a small entrance. The passageway is long, low and ill-lit, the torches guttering in the current of cold air that streams along it. At the end, we enter a meagre round chamber where an inadequate fire smoulders in the grate. As I walk around, trying to force an appreciative comment, I create a draught, and smoke billows into the room. I suppress a cough.

"This will serve me very well," I smile bravely, wishing with all my heart it were true. Myfanwy, who is not so schooled in hiding her feelings, asks indignantly, "And where is my lady to sleep, and her attendants?"

"Oh, there is another chamber. There are several rooms linked by passageways. When I am in residence I use them myself but I thought they would serve you better, Margaret."

With no little relief I follow him along the passage to another room, almost identical. Unable to find an honest thing to say in praise of the accommodation I kneel on the window seat and look out across the river. To the left is what looks like a religious house.

"What is that place, Jasper? Is it an abbey?"

He moves close to me and leans to the window, a hand on my shoulder.

"It is Monkton Priory; the Benedictines there do good works among the local poor."

Relieved that God's presence is discernible in this wild, forsaken place, I try to look happy.

Turning to face me, Jasper adds, "The church is dedicated to St Nicholas who, I think, is your favourite saint."

I am startled that he should recall so small a personal detail, but I do not comment. He holds out his hand and helps me to my feet. I survey the small bed, the truckle bed beneath, the seat at the hearth and feel a twist of guilt at turning him from his quarters.

"But where will you lodge, Jasper? I am sorry for stealing your rooms."

"It is my pleasure, Margaret. I am bereft of a brother, yet soon you are to bless me with a nephew or, perhaps, a niece. I will do all in my power for your comfort. If there is anything you lack, just send for me, day or night."

He bends over my hand, his lips not brushing my skin as they usually do, but warm on my wrist. When he straightens, we look into each other's eyes and acknowledge our shared sorrow.

Myfanwy, seemingly attacked by a sudden spate of coughing, breaks our reverie. She bends over, thumping her chest, her eyes watering.

"Fetch a pitcher of water, Ned," I say, my concern for Myfanwy overcoming my own worries. I go to her side, pat her ineffectually on the back while Ned brings a slopping jug of water and splashes some into a cup.

"Thank you," I say as I pass it to Myfanwy. "You were very swift, Ned."

I watch anxiously while she takes small sips, her colour slowly returning to normal. When she is fully restored and breathing normally again, I turn to resume my conversation with Jasper. But he has gone.

We retire to bed early, but I sleep ill in the hard, narrow bed. I lie flat on my back, feeling the child squirm as he seeks a better position. Edmund should be here with me. He used to love to follow the contours of the baby's movements, put his ear to my belly to see if he could hear anything within. We spent long hours of the night imagining our firstborn's face, what his voice would be like, what shade his hair. I was safe in my husband's care and our relationship showed such promise. I try not to dwell on that one time when our mutual love for our child led to other, unexpected things. My chest grows tight with longing for the act that will never now be repeated. Now, Edmund will never look upon our child's face, and my firstborn will be his last.

I heave myself onto my side and stare into the darkness. I have never felt this afraid before, or this alone, but now I am lost among comparative strangers in a foreign land.

Duty dictates that I write to my mother. I am at a loss as to what to write and in the end send a brief note, outlying what has befallen me. I do not want her to come here; having been my own mistress for so long I could not bear to live beneath her jurisdiction again. It would be nice to see Edith, but she is recently wed and soon to have a child of her own. She will not want to leave her home to be with me. All I can do is write to her, but I can never put what I really feel into a letter, and I know that anything I tell Edith will be related straight away to Mother.

Mother is not tardy in sending her reply. "You must come home, Margaret," she urges. "Your place is with me; you will be safe here and we can raise your child in the nursery, just as you were raised." I ponder the idea for no more than a moment. The scenario flits across my mind's eye; I see myself living under her roof, a young widow, the child in her nursery evidence of my fertility. Once more, she would place me on the marriage market, and wave my fortune beneath the noses of those hungry for power. I have no wish to see her and will not go. Too much has passed since she sent me away, and Edmund left me in no doubt as to his private opinion of her. I am a woman now, and it has become very clear that she desires only the benefits I can provide.

My child and I share a close relationship with the king but I am determined we will never be an asset to her. Edmund would have forbidden it. One by one, she has arranged advantageous marriages for my siblings; each one a benefit to her own ambition. Without hesitation, she sold me in marriage when I was still a child, and gave no heed to the sort of man I was marrying. She gave no thought to what I might encounter once I left her household and she sent me into the world unschooled in the nature of marriage. Only by chance was Edmund a worthy man, a young man with enough kindness in his heart to treat the child he married well. He was a good husband, but that good fortune owed no thanks to my mother.

My outraged pen rushes across the page in a scrawl of misery. Afterwards, when I read the words I have written, I realise my own bitterness and do not send it after all. But the exercise does me some good, as if the act of scratching my broken hopes and dreams onto a piece of parchment and sealing it with self-pitying tears provides a kind of healing. I have no idea how or why the act of writing it down is so soothing, but although I am still broken and afraid, having purged my mind, I am able to function again. With a little more courage than I had before, I agree that plans should be laid in place for my coming confinement.

A week or so later Ned brings me another letter, this time in Edith's hand.

Dearest Margaret, she writes.

I am so sorry to learn of your misfortune. We miss you so much, Margaret. Why do you not return home, if not to Mother at Bletsoe, then here with me? My husband is a good man and says he will be glad to welcome you. You should be among your own at this sad time, to bring your child forth in safety and comfort rather than some far flung barbarian place.

I have a room prepared for you, a large one with a view across the parkland. It will be such fun, Margaret, we can sew baby clothes together and raise our sons in the same nursery and oh, so much else.

Please, write to me as soon as you can so that I may put the wheels in motion. I so look forward to seeing you again, you have always been my dearest sister.

I let the letter fall into my lap. I have no desire to return to England. After running my own household I will never allow myself to become a guest in my sister's house. It is better that I remain here at Pembroke, where I am, more or less, my own mistress. Edith will never see me as an adult. She would simper and stroke my hair and treat me like some precious puppy. It is better here in the chills of Pembroke than the false welcome of my mother's house, or the cosy comforts of my sister's.

I do not form a reply. I leave the letter unanswered; it remains on my table, the words resounding in my mind like the temptation of the devil. The parchment yellows more each day, and begins to curl at the edges until one of my women asks if she can dispose of it.

I think for a long moment. It is my last chance. If I do not send a reply and dispose of it, I forego the opportunity of turning back the years and re-entering the security of my nursery days. Yet, now that I think of it, those days were not secure at all. My mother was not bringing up a child; she gave no thought to me. She was raising a bride, a prize to barter for a pot of gold, an icon of power to raise her status and buy favour with the king. Can I be sure Edith's motives are any different? I nod my head slowly, and without hesitation, she thrusts the letter into the flames.

The edges of the parchment darken and shrivel, the marks of Edith's dubious affection turning brown and withering to ashes.

Someone offers me a cup, and I smile up at them before placing the cold rim against my lips, the wine rich upon my tongue. Pembroke is where I belong. It is what Edmund would have wanted and it is where I am determined to stay.

Pembroke Castle – January 1457

My belly is vast. I wonder that human skin can stretch to encompass such a thing. The child is very quiet now and I sometimes worry that I have lost him. Filled with horror, I poke and prod at my abdomen until he squirms away from my prying fingers.

If I were at my mother's house, I would have been locked away from the rest of the world a month since but here at Pembroke, although some provisions have been made, I am free to walk on the parapet, or look out of the window toward the river and the church on the hill. I am not sorry to dispense with etiquette; the idea of being incarcerated in those tiny chambers for weeks on end is not a welcome one.

I miss the gardens of Lamphey but there are none here, not even produce is grown; vegetables are ferried across from the priory to accompany the endless round of goose, capon and salmon that we are served at table. I have a sudden memory of the rich fayre I enjoyed during my visit to court when I was a girl. I recall an immense pie shaped like a castle, filled with rich, meaty sauce. The king and queen probably eat like that every day while I must survive on plainer fayre. I have been so long in Wales, so completely over taken by the events that have befallen me, I wonder if I will ever return to England, or ever visit the royal court again. I should like the king to bless my child, one day.

I turn listlessly from the window. Ever since we rode here from Carmarthen, I have lacked energy, lacked joy. It is as if a thick mist has descended upon me and I cannot see my way ahead. I know the birth must be soon, there is no escaping that, but what shall come after?

My future that a few months ago seemed so solid is now like slurry beneath my feet. I do not know what to do and God, despite my constant prayer, remains stubbornly silent. While I was prostrate with sorrow and fear, Jasper, even in his own grief, arranged everything. Perhaps he has a plan for me, also. Edmund has been laid to rest at Grey Friars, close to where he died. I have not seen the burial place but I picture him sealed in a tomb for all eternity, his brilliance fading as I grow old and the memory of our love becomes dim.

I cannot imagine the vibrancy he owned vanquished by death, his golden hair beginning to dull, his eyes soon to hollow, his skin to dry and flake until all he was becomes dust. Death must come to us all but my macabre thoughts make me gasp. I shake my head to dispel the image. I must put away the resentment I feel and thank God that, for all eternity, masses will be said for Edmund's soul. Jasper and I have paid the Grey Friars a small fortune to ensure it is so. When my own time comes, I will leave instruction that my body be laid beside his. I cannot imagine ever loving another.

In my loneliness, the façade of strength I had so briefly conjured fades fast. Each night, when darkness falls, my despair erupts again; it rises like a tide, gushing from some place deep inside me until I am consumed and fall weeping onto my pillows. I wake each morning drenched in tears, both for myself and my poor fatherless child. Listlessly, I seek direction from someone wiser than myself, searching for someone to show me the path I must follow. I am forever on my knees beseeching God's help, begging for a light to show me the way.

When it all becomes too much to bear, I try to stave off the overwhelming misery by retreating into a childish game, in which Edmund is away, fighting for the king, and will be home with me come supper time. It is only such small silly things that help me through.

By the time January arrives, the weather is bitter cold, and there is little comfort to be had inside the castle. Although the fire is built high, ice forms on the inside of the windows at night, and draughts whip along the passage, seeking a way past the thick tapestry that screens the door. I am constantly cold, constantly miserable.

In the worst weather, we keep the shutters closed and pull our seats as close to the fire as we safely can. It is a gloomy, mole-like existence. Myfanwy tries to keep me entertained with chatter, bringing gossip from the castle kitchens to my chamber, but I do not care for it. I bend over my sewing, adding hundreds of tiny stitches while her voice fills my head and the birthing chair waits, like a portent of doom, in the corner.

Whenever I am alone, I pray to St Nicholas, who has helped me so often in the past, and to St Margaret, who keeps watch over all women in childbirth. I can no longer bear to look at my own body; the fear of what must surely come robs me of sleep, robs me of peace, and fills me with terror.

I am so very small, my arms and legs are thin, easily bruised, and my knees are knobbly and red from praying. The child inside makes a monster of me; my huge abdomen and swollen breasts seem absurd against the rest of my body.

I know the facts of what is to happen to me. I have seen pups and foals born and know the path the child must take, but I can make no sense of it. How a baby, even a small one, can come forth from me in such a way is both bewildering and terrifying. My child is trapped within me, and we are both confined inside a strange castle, in an alien land, while the monsters outside creep ever closer.

The women think I do not hear them whisper about the dangers my slight stature may impose. They think I haven't seen the midwife shake her head and purse her lips.

"She is very small," she whispers when she thinks I am out of ear shot, and her words echo around my head like the tolling of the plague bell. Death sits at every window, a hungry smirk on his face as he waits to take me.

<u>Pembroke Castle – January 28th 1457</u>

Something disturbs me. I open my eyes but the night candle has burned out and I can see nothing in the darkness. "Myfanwy?" I sit up, call her name again but know instinctively that I am alone.

She has been absent often lately. She thinks I have not noticed, but as my pregnancy progresses, I wake in the darkest hours of the night and find her bed empty. I blink into blackness. The candle has burned out but there is, as yet, no sign of morning. Something is wrong.

Fingers of fear flutter in my belly. I throw back the cover and slide from the mattress, feeling my way across the freezing room. I grope on Myfanwy's truckle bed – the rumpled sheets are cold to the touch. As I had guessed, she has been gone for some time. Fumbling for a light, I call out for her and as I do so, something grips the base of my spine. Pain radiates right through me, stealing my breath as my belly is tied into knots. I freeze, paralysed in agony until it passes.

"Myfanwy!" I gasp again as soon as I can breathe. I reach for the door and throw it open. I call her name again and, when no answer comes, I call for Ned, screaming like a fishwife along the passage.

Where is everyone?

"My lady?" Ned emerges from a niche where he has made his bed with Jay. The boy coughs and yawns, rubs his eye. "Are you ill, my lady? Is it ... is it the baby?" His horrified eyes trickle down to my belly, widening as he notices the spreading patch of dampness on my shift.

"Where is everyone? Where is Myfanwy?"

"I will fetch her ..."

"No. Don't leave me, not yet."

I can feel another pain, unimaginably agonising, rising rapidly from some unknown quarter of my body. I grasp his arm, lean over, my other hand to my back, biting my lip in an effort not to cry out.

I am afraid. I want Myfanwy. I want Edmund. I would even welcome the presence of my mother.

"I will help you back to the chamber."

I grab his arm and make no protest when he places his hand about my waist and bids me lean on him. I walk like an ancient woman, my knees palsied, each step a torment. His fingers strike cold through my thin night gown, the sweaty, smoky aroma of his hair assaulting my nose. Intimacy with an underling does not concern me now. Other fears loom large in my mind; memories of the women I have known who have died bringing forth a child. Their sorrowful faces float across my mind, but I push them away. I must not think of them now. I am not them. I am Margaret.

With my arm draped about his shoulder, I allow Ned to lead me slowly back to bed. He helps me onto the mattress, carefully lifts my legs and covers them, plumps the pillow. "Will you be all right now, my lady? Shall I run and fetch Myfanwy and the midwife?"

"They should be here – everything was made ready. They had their orders ..."

Another pain rises unbidden, and I close my eyes shutting out Ned's terror-stricken face, my teeth clenched on my bottom lip. I have never known, or imagined, pain like it. When the agony lessens, I nod at him and try to smile, try to speak normally. "Yes, fetch them, please."

"I will bring the Earl, too," he yells as he scoots from the chamber.

Oh no, please. Not Jasper. Anyone but him.

What seems like an age later they burst into my chamber. Myfanwy rushes to the bed. "Oh, Margaret, I am so sorry, I should have been here. I am so sorry."

I see her as if in a dream, certain details striking through my pain. She is clad only in her shift, her face is flushed, her lips strangely swollen, and there is a mark on her throat like a large round bruise.

"Where have you been?"

"Come; let me bathe your face. The midwife will be here any minute, she will instruct us further."

"Fetch more fuel for the fire." Jasper has arrived and sends Ned hurrying away again. He takes one step closer to the bed. He is dishevelled, as if his clothes have been thrown on anyhow, his hair damp and standing on end.

"Help me sit up," I say, and when Myfanwy struggles to lift me, he comes forward. His strong arm slides beneath me as the pain assaults me again. I cling to his shirt, bury my face in his shoulder, and he holds me while I grit my teeth, fighting for breath, my body rigid from the attack. When the moment passes, I lie limp for a moment, glad of his strong arms, his musty male odour. Then my eyes snap open as suddenly everything becomes clear.

His skin, his personal aroma, is laced with something else, some*body* else. Myfanwy; it is clear he has been with her for he reeks of the scent of their mating. While I have been drowning in grief and fear, almost giving birth to my son with only a boy to attend me, my best friend and my protector, heedless of my needs, have crept away like thieves in the night to satisfy their lust.

But I cannot worry about that now and I tuck my resentment away.

Jasper calls Jay to his side and he and Ned slip from the room. They have no place in a lying-in chamber. The tiny apartment fills with women, half-dressed and still fugged with sleep as they fuss with unguents and potions. The midwife orders the heavy birthing chair to be dragged closer to the fire. With fear bubbling like vomit in my belly, I stare at it as if it is an instrument of torture.

They leave me to my own devices while they rush around, calling instructions to each other, frantically getting all in order; things that should have been done before. The midwife asks me to lie on the bed and, after a cursory examination, she says, "You'll do for a while, my lady. You've a way to go yet."

My heart sinks. 'A way to go?' I am not sure I can bear this much longer. It is worse than anything I have ever known; far worse than my monthly cramps, far worse than the measles, or the time I fell in the garden and broke my littlest finger. It must be less painful to be shot through the heart by an arrow, or torn apart by horses. I want to whimper, I want to cry like a baby for my nurse but I am a lady, and the Countess of Richmond. I cannot wail like a commoner... I bite down on my pillow as another pain slides up from my nethers.

The women are warming towels at the hearth. "Aaaahhhhh!" At my scream, their heads turn. Myfanwy drops her towel and climbs onto the bed beside me. I grip her wrist.

"God help me, Myfanwy. I have not even the strength of mind to pray ..."

She wipes sweat from my brow, trickles water between my lips.

"The midwife says it is normal, Margaret. It shouldn't be much longer. Think of holding your child in a little while, your little 'Owain', and hold onto that thought."

I am given little relief between assaults of pain. I can feel it coming. First it is little more than a slight niggle in my back, but it grows in intensity, running across my body like a flowing tide until it consumes me entirely. My belly tightens, my back bone is ready to snap, my whole being under attack. I thrash around on the bed, battling to escape it, although some part of me knows the pain is part of me. I can never escape myself.

I am lost; tossed on a sea of agony, coming to only when the pain is at its height, and lapsing into blackness as it eases. I cry for my mother, ask for my old nurse who has lain in her grave for many a year. For hours, I hover between this world and the next, at the mercy of God to whom I am too torn to pray. Somewhere above me, ghostly voices whisper; they speak hopelessly of travail. They speak of death; they speak of a poor motherless babe whose heart ceases to beat before he can take his first breath.

It seems like hours later when the midwife orders the women to move me. Through a haze of pain I am carried to the birthing chair. My shift is soaked with blood and birth fluid, it flaps cold about my legs until they strip it from me. Although the fire is blazing I start to shiver, I cannot get warm. I stare blankly at someone, a woman who grasps my hands and screams at me for pity's sake to stay awake.

It is Myfanwy. I grab her shift and try to focus on her face, refusing to let go. She rubs my arms to encourage my blood to flow, peering at me through dank, tousled hair, her smile like the grimace of a death mask. But I cannot respond. I am aware that soon the pain will come again and I am not sure I can survive it. I have little fight left, and although my body is wracked and my mind tortured, I know it is not yet over. There will be worse to come.

A bell rings somewhere in the castle, and to my broken spirits it is clear they are ringing my death knell. Naked now, all modesty abandoned, I stare down at my body, my straining stomach and my bony bloodstained knees, and feel the now familiar twinge in my lower spine. I don't want it to come; I fight to repel it, twist in their arms, trying to stop it from taking hold of me.

From somewhere between my knees, the midwife wrenches my thighs apart and yells, "Push with the next pain, my lady; push with all your might."

At first I do not know what she means. How should I push? What should I push with? I grope for Myfanwy's hand and as the pain increases, I instinctively duck my head to my chest and bear down with all my strength. I hear my teeth crack, I grunt and groan and strain, but nothing happens.

The pain grows worse, my womb is squeezed until I think I will burst, and then mercifully it begins to abate. I let my head fall back, sink into darkness until Myfanwy douses me with water. She trickles it over my forehead, into my mouth, daubs it upon my neck and breast. I spring awake, gasp for breath. Perhaps it is better to perish now than to carry on. I try to pant a last goodbye.

The midwife counts my breathing, puts her head to my chest, listens … for something. I thrust her away. The monsters are coming again. I try to fight them but they have broken in from the garden, they have laid hold of me and are rending my body in two, tearing me to pieces.

Someone is screaming.

"Hush, my lady, you will bring down the castle." The voice comes from far away. I open my eyes, just a slit, and their faces sway and blur before me. They give me water and I gulp it down, it trickles down my chin and trails like icy fingers across my breast. I want to sleep, I want to die but the beast is coming again. I can hear his footstep, feel his sharp teeth, his claws dig deep inside me, tearing my skin, ripping my sinew, breaking my bones.

Someone is screaming.

"The child is misaligned. They might not come through this."

"Neither of them? You must do something."

Voices float above me, words I cannot comprehend, a language I do not recognise. Fingers probe with big hairy, clawed nails. There are many monsters now; they invade my body, cutting into me. They are stealing my child, taking my baby. Myfanwy is praying, praying for my life. It is small comfort.

Someone is screaming.

I am consumed. All I know is pain, back breaking, loin-tearing pain. I am pulled up, forced to sit bolt upright, they trap my arms, hold me fast. I cannot move. I am paralysed. I am lost.

A dozen hands upon me, they keep me down, and my thighs are dragged so wide that my hips are breaking. I scream as they tear the child from me. The monsters sever the cord that binds us and I suffer sharp bereavement as they bear away a tiny, pale blue, limp body. I fall back into a pool of blood and birth fluid, the acrid stench of it thick in the air. As I close my eyes, I hear the thin high wail of my grieving women. Darkness, impenetrable blackness swims at the periphery of my mind; it is growing deeper, darker. It is rushing in to blind me. I fall into deep dark blood.

All is black.

When I open my eyes and try to move, pain shoots through my body. I whimper and fall back on the pillow, and a shadow falls across the bed.

"Margaret, thank goodness. I thought you would never wake." Myfanwy takes my hand. "How are you feeling?"

"I don't know." My voice croaks, I run my tongue across parched lips. "Can I have some water?"

She brings a cup and as she helps me drink, the door opens and the midwife comes in. She stands at the foot of the bed, hands on hips, and surveys me for a while.

"We thought we'd lost you at one point, my lady. I must examine you when you've refreshed yourself. Do you have any pain?"

I shake my head, but it isn't true. It would be easier to list the parts of me that don't hurt. I feel bruised from head to foot, my nether regions are throbbing and sore, my limbs and joints aching. As the midwife leaves us, promising to return shortly, I try to shift on the mattress. As I move, a rush of warm liquid gushes from me and I realise my private parts are swathed in wadding and bandages. I send Myfanwy a questioning look. She pulls a face, her cheeks growing pink.

"As I understand it, the child was attempting to be born before your womb was fully open." She turns scarlet. "You should let the midwife explain, Margaret, but, it seems your womb was torn during the violent nature of the birth. There was so much blood. We thought you would not recover. I cannot tell you how glad I am."

She mops away a tear. My hands fall heavily on the blankets as she releases me and turns away. I look at her long hair trailing down her back.

"Did the child breathe at all?"

Since I can hardly bear to ask it, I speak to her while she is turned away dreading her reply. She halts suddenly and turns again, her face turning scarlet as she comes rushing to the bed to seize my hands.

"Margaret? Margaret, he not only breathed; he is breathing still! He is in the next chamber with the wet nurse. He is tiny but very nicely formed and growing stronger by the minute. I will have him brought to you right away."

My heart falters, skips a few beats; my breath halts in my throat. He lives! How is it possible? How could a tiny scrap of life endure what we both suffered? It is a wonder I survived myself.

The great knot of sorrow that has been wedged in the base of my throat is suddenly released, and I am crying with great painful sobs. Huge tears splash upon my cheeks and fall upon the counterpane. My mouth is squared, my nose beginning to run.

"Oh, Myfanwy," I wail through snot and tears, "I gave up hope that he would live. Somewhere in the midst of all that pain I lost hope. I was certain we would both perish."

The door opens and the midwife enters carrying a tightly wrapped bundle.

"Now, now," she says, her smile as wide as a church door. "We mustn't have tears. I've a young man wanting to meet his mother."

She comes forward. I dash the moisture from my face with the back of my hand and open my arms to embrace my son; Edmund's son.

My bruised and broken body is forgotten as I look down at him through a blur of happy tears. He is red and wrinkled, a large blue bruise beginning to spread across his forehead.

"We had to be a little rough with him in the end, my lady. But we brought him forth safe and sound. He will soon be good as new."

Within the cocoon of swaddling bands his face is a round, red ball. A few strands of dark red hair peek from the blanket. His mouth is pursed, making gentle sucking motion, a crease between his brows. Delicate half-moon lashes rest on his cheeks.

With a tentative finger, I stroke the curve of his cheek and my heart swells. My body is wracked and ruined and by rights I should be dead, yet here I am, alive and well and holding my son. He is small, but thriving. For the first time I have done something right, made my mark on the world. Now, I have a reason to live, something to smile about, and someone to love. I will never be lonely again.

Pembroke Castle – February 1457

For many weeks I do not think of the future. I live in the here and now, concentrating on healing and bonding with my son. But one morning, after breaking my fast, I go with Myfanwy and Jasper to the chapel. The world outside is locked in a frozen white shroud, but inside the chapel, where the sun's meagre warmth cannot reach, the cold seems even more intense. The only comfort is the gleam of God's light through the eastern window, the multitude of candles, and the voices of the choir.

After giving praise to God, we stand in a ring beside the priest while he breaks the ice on the font and trickles holy water over my son's head.

"What is the child to be called?" the priest asks, and Jasper looks up, his voice loud and echoing in the nave. "Owain," he says.

But then time seems to falter and I hear another voice, an instruction spoken in deep, masculine tones. At first I think it is God's voice, or one of his angels, but then, when the words come again, I recognise it as belonging to someone much dearer. Alert, I stare from Jasper to the priest to Myfanwy, but their faces are lit with holy adoration and none of them gives any indication they have heard anything.

"Name him Henry," the urgent whisper comes again. I am flooded with warmth, as if Edmund is wrapping me in his arms and breathing into my ear. I shuffle my feet, clear my throat, lean forward and place a restraining hand on the sleeve of the priest's robe. He looks at me with surprise, unused to hindrance from one as young as I.

"No, not Owain," I say, my breath short and sharp, surprised at my own instruction. "Name him Henry; it was his father's wish."

As one, my companions turn and stare at me, making a child of me again.

"Henry? But you said he was to be Owain; it was all agreed." Jasper is frowning, willing me to change my mind and name my son for his grandfather, Owain Tudor. But I opt to listen to a higher authority.

"I was wrong. I had forgotten," I stammer, "but I remember now. Edmund told me before he rode away that he wanted his son to be called Henry, in honour of his brother, the king."

Afterwards, when they have left me to sleep, I take the child from his cradle and slip away from the chamber. It is icy cold but bright on the parapet wall, the air tainted with the smoke of many fires. Below me, the household bustles around as usual, to all intents and purposes a normal day. The blacksmith's hammer steadily marks the passing minutes, the honking geese are setting up a din. Oblivious of my presence so high above her, a girl runs across the ward, slopping milk from her buckets in her haste.

The sun is as high as it gets in February. I stroll slowly along the edge of the wall, in love with the bright blue world, smiling at the slow moving river, the sleepy priory buildings across the way. I pause, and as if missing the motion, the child stirs in my arms and nuzzles into my bony chest. He is hungry again, but my body has no nourishment for him. Soon, I will take him below and seek the services of his wet nurse. For now, to pacify him, I raise him to my face and kiss him again, his cheek warm and smelling of milk. I can never bestow enough love on my Henry.

So many years lay ahead, so many trials, so many potential dangers to be faced without a father. I feel the now familiar creeping shrim of fear, but it is quickly dispelled. Since his christening, and his acceptance into God's holy church, I feel more at peace. God loves Henry, I can sense it, and with Jasper as his godfather, he now has a guardian both in Heaven and on Earth.

Jasper has promised to ensure Henry is well schooled and protected, and I will see it is so. Between us, Jasper and I will keep him safe. He will thrive, be happy, and learn all there is for a man to know. He will be wise in knowledge, gracious at court, and fierce in battle; an asset to his family and to his king.

There has never been anyone so precious to me. I lift Henry to my cheek again, inhale his infant scent, close my eyes, and dream of all he will become, all he will achieve.

"My Lady Margaret, you must come inside, you will both perish out there!" When the voice calls to me from inside, I do not answer at once. Instead, I close my eyes and send up a prayer of thanks to Heaven. As I stand there embracing my son, I am aware of God's presence. His blessing washes over me. I know Edmund is at his side and both of them are whispering, "Margaret, you have done well."

I walk through cries of hostility, people tug at my clothes, spit on my gown. "Witch," they cry. "Devil's whore!" Their hatred is deafening. Behind me, an armoured man pushes me along a path I must not tread. I stumble, wrenching my ankle, and cry out at the sudden pain.

A missile flies from the crowd and strikes me in the mouth. I taste blood, my lip swelling, futile tears soaking my cheeks. I twist and turn in their grip, crossing my arms in a vain attempt to protect myself. Ignoring my protest, they tear away my gown, leaving only my shift, and force me to climb to a pinnacle I have no wish to reach. Rough hands thrust me hard against the stake, my arms are wrenched backwards, my wrists bound cruelly tight. There is no sign of God. Still the crowd call out against me, naming me a traitor to Heaven, a traitor to the crown.

"Edmund!" I cry, repeating his name over and over until I remember he cannot help me. "Jasper!" I change my plea, "where are you?" And then I glimpse his golden hair, the familiar cut of his figure, and relief surges through me. He has come, he will keep me safe. I close my eyes and thank God before opening them again.

Jasper is standing a little apart from the crowd, his arms folded, a mocking smile on his face. I realise he is not my friend. He promised to care for me, to protect my child, my Henry. Anger adds its helplessness to my fear. "Jasper!" I scream his name louder, knowing I am betrayed.

The man behind me pulls tighter on the rope that binds me.

"Now, now, Joan, that ain't lady-like."

"Joan? I am not Joan, I am Margaret!"

He pushes his face close to mine; his stagnant breath, the filth of his clogged pores, the coarse hairs on the end of his nose adding to my nightmare. From the corner of my eye

148

I see a trio of men surge forward; demons with lighted torches.

"Please," I wail, although I know it will do no good. "There has been a mistake. I am not Joan. I am Margaret."

He laughs, turns away, and I watch in horror as a tiny flame ignites and begins to creep steadily up the faggots. An acrid smell of smoke brings the memory of autumn, the stench of death and decay. My head rolls back, I close my eyes and scream at Heaven.

Blood trickles down my chin, the flow increasing until it drips onto my chest, soaks into my shift, trickles down, hissing into the flames, across the ground between my tormentors' feet, soaking into the very sod itself.

I am one with England and with my death ...

"My Lady, my lady, wake up. It is just a dream ... oh my goodness, you have bitten right through your lip."

Myfanwy leans over me, her hair tumbling, her sweet blessed arms pulling me from the suffocating pillow. I cling to her, my tears and blood tarnishing her pristine linen as, like a mother, she strokes my hair. "It was just a dream," she murmurs, "only a dream."

I rest on her shoulder and stare into the lurking shadows in the corner of the chamber, the horror of the nightmare slow to leave me. Gradually, as my sobs abate, her rocking stills and she pulls away. "What was it, Margaret? Can you tell me?"

I shake my head.

I can never speak of it.

The dreams have been coming to me nightly. Dreams in which I am not myself, not in control of my own destiny; dreams where I am at the mercy of faceless enemies. The childhood obsession I had with Joan d'Arc usurps my very self, and while I sleep our souls somehow merge.

"It was just a silly dream."

Myfanwy stands over me while I sip a cup of milk and honey through sore lips. She begins to babble about the day ahead, throws open the shutters to let in the blue March daylight to chase the darkness away. I try to brush off the nightmare but it lingers; every so often throughout the day it returns like a dour dark cloud shutting out the sun.

The euphoria I felt after Henry's birth did not last long, and it has been replaced by a heavy shroud of sorrow and misery. I am out of step with life, and lack the spirit to move boldly into the future.

Myfanwy's strategy is to distract me from my gloom; she tries to tear away the thick woolly veil that seems to lie between me and the rest of the world. She fails. I do not care about the approach of spring, or the plight of the poor, or the germinating seeds on her windowsill. I only care about Henry.

He is thriving, growing well under the ministrations of his wet nurse. I bite my lip in envy when he snuggles at her breast, drawing life and sustenance, but even if it were appropriate for me to nurse him myself, my paps have shrivelled so small that in order to present a womanly shape, I am forced to pad my bodice once more. At least my son is flourishing. I have no worries on that score, although I am increasingly concerned for his future, for my own future. Everything seems so very bleak.

As the country falls further into disarray, Jasper's expression grows grimmer. The king's ailment continues and the queen refuses to leave her refuge in the midlands; she fills Kenilworth with arms, surrounds herself with supporters. She misgoverns the country and makes herself no friends. York and Warwick are now openly hostile, and those loyal to the king are torn, reluctant to support the queen, who now styles herself as regent.

One evening, after supper in Pembroke's great hall, Jasper asks that I spare him a few moments. Myfanwy makes to leave us but Jasper calls her back. "Nay, Myfanwy, stay please. You should hear this. Margaret will be glad of your counsel."

Her cheeks flush red but she looks pleased as she takes her place beside me, carefully spreading her skirts and placing her hands genteelly in her lap. I have the suspicion that she is perfectly aware of what is to come. Alert and ready for ill news, I try to prepare myself for whatever he is about to say.

Jasper paces the floor in front of the hearth. "Margaret, the time has come to look to your future protection. I – my jurisdiction is spreading and my duties will soon take me away from here for long periods of time."

I open my mouth to speak, but he holds up a hand to silence me and I subside, trying to stem the anxiety that bubbles in my stomach.

He is going to send me away.

"Although I will always continue to care for and guard the interests of both you and Henry, I feel you need another protector, a husband who will provide day to day security."

"A husband? I am only just widowed. I am not ready to marry again!"

He sighs. Myfanwy fidgets in her seat.

"It cannot be helped, Margaret. You must just make the best of things."

I realise my future has been discussed between them, probably during the long dark night in the secrecy of their sinfulness. With a pang of jealousy for their intimacy, I tighten my lips.

"Who? Who do you have in mind?"

"Obviously, we will undertake no match that does not meet with your approval."

His reluctance to name the man who has so obviously already been selected deepens my concern.

"But - but I like it here. Henry and I are as safe within this fortress as we can possibly be, nothing can touch us here. You will protect us, I know that. Jasper ... why ... why don't we marry?"

Silence falls like a heavy curtain and then Myfanwy squeaks and puts out a hand, shaking her head, biting her lip in reproach.

"Oh, Margaret!" she mutters, her cheeks pink. "How could you?"

Jasper shakes himself, stammers to find his voice.

"Margaret ... you are my brother's wife. That could never be."

"We could go to the king, your brother, and ask him to seek a dispensation. It is what Edmund would want."

He looks at me in horror, like a man trying to tell a little girl that the sweetmeats have all been eaten. "Besides," he ends lamely, "I ... I have no wish to marry."

"Well, I am not pretending it would be a love match, but we are friends ..." I lapse into embarrassed silence and wish I had not spoken.

I look from him to Myfanwy, who has now turned her body a little away from me and is examining a loose thread on the tapestry seat beside her. I realise too late the gaucheness of my outburst. I have spoken out of turn and we are all discomforted by it.

"Well, who then? Who will wish to marry me? The physician has made it clear I am unlikely to bear another child. Who will want to ally themselves with a plain and barren wife? Tell me that!"

Jasper gives a snort of disbelief.

"Do you really have no idea how rich you are? How your connections with the king make you a desirable prize on the marriage market? For Heaven's sake, child, barren or not, the right man would take you far away from here, provide you with a life at court such as you deserve. He would ply you with jewels and dainties and fine gowns ... you will never get that buried in Wales with me."

"What about Henry? Will he have a place in this hypothetical husband's household? Will he be welcome at court?"

A long silence. Jasper looks at the ceiling and then into the hearth. My heart thumps as I wait for him to speak.

"Henry will stay with me ... but the marriage won't take place for a long time. You can stay with him until your period of mourning is over; you will see him weaned and walking long before you go."

Dread washes over me. I leap to my feet, my stomach churning. *Little Henry, weaned and walking.* I raise my head, letting Jasper see the tears in my eyes, the pain in my heart.

"I would rather spend each day with my son; share each moment of his life until he is a man with his own household, his own wife; and then I would share his children too."

"Gahh!" Jasper makes an impatient movement. "That never happens. You know that. All boys are sent away to be raised in the household of a knight; they never stay at home with their mothers. Be glad he will be with me, and not with strangers. Why should your son be any different?"

"Because he is the only son I shall ever have. Henry is all I will ever have. He is my life."

Another long silence. I stare at Jasper, willing him to relent, to tell me he was wrong, that he will rethink the situation. Instead, he turns away, puts a hand on the mantel and stares angrily into the flames.

"You are to accompany me to the Duke of Buckingham's residence at Greenfield near Newport. It isn't far. Once there, you will make the acquaintance of Harry Stafford, the duke's second-born son. He is an amiable fellow. Try to like him a little; it will make things easier for you."

Jasper abruptly crosses the room. As he nears my chair, I leap to my feet, grab his sleeve.

"Jasper, my lord; if … if I cannot like him … you will not force me … please, at least promise me that much."

He stares into my face with eyes so much like Edmund's, I could weep. His mouth softens, and a smile plays at the corners of his mouth.

"Nay, Margaret. I will not force you – you have my promise. This time, your bridegroom will be of your own choosing. Look upon this meeting as an introduction, no more, but think on it, be wise and look to your future security. Use your mind, not your foolish heart."

It is happening again. For all Jasper's assurances, my life is out of my hands. I know that my marriage to Buckingham's son is a foregone conclusion. Just like the dream in which I am burned for a witch, my hands bound, my wishes ignored, my dreams ashes. It is my fate.

A brisk cold wind blows against our faces as we travel east to Newport. After taking leave of Henry and regaling Myfanwy, who is feeling sickly, with a thousand instructions as to his well being, my heart is heavy. As we ride ever farther from Pembroke, my spirits decline even more, the chill damp weather making my nose run. I huddle deep into my cloak and keep my eyes on the muddy road that I have no wish to travel. After several attempts to cheer me by engaging me in conversation Jasper falls silent. A short time later, frustrated by my stubborn sulks, he kicks his mount forward and strikes up a conversation with one of his men.

I shrink into my own misery, wrap myself in gloom, wishing I had never been born; or at least wishing I had been born a boy, in charge of my own destiny.

To pass the time, I try to recall all I know of the Duke of Buckingham. He is a powerful man, of course, and one not given to keeping his own counsel. I seem to remember Jasper saying he was not an admirer of the queen, but his loyalty to the king precluded him from turning against her. As a result, he has fallen foul of Warwick and York, whose activities he renounces as treason.

I picture a large, forceful man, brutish and lordly, and imagine his son will be made in his father's image. It is with great trepidation that, after almost two days on the road, we approach the estate at Greenfields. This visit could prove pivotal in my life; if fate is against me, I could ride away from here the betrothed bride of a brute.

At least today is brighter than yesterday, and the sunshine goes some way toward lifting my sense of doom. As we near our destination, I notice a group of lent lilies dancing in the hedgerow, primroses emerging from last year's decaying leaves. It is not easy to be dour on such a pleasant day. For the first time in months, my spirits stir a little; perhaps Jasper is right and it is up to me to take my life and make of it the best I can.

The gatehouse is thrown open in anticipation of our arrival; we ride into the bailey where Jasper dismounts quickly. He spins on his heel, puts out a hand to help me alight, but a groom is there before him. He leads my mare to the mounting block and reaches up to steady me.

I grasp the groom's arms and slide to the ground before dismissing him with a wave of my hand, and turning my attention to brushing my skirts and straightening my veil. The groom bows and gestures toward the hall. Taking Jasper's proffered arm, I allow him to lead me into the house.

After the brightness of the day, it seems dark inside. I blink, trying to adjust my vision, and look about the oak panelled hall at the vast tapestries and a wide-mouthed hearth with a huge fire blazing. This is one of the duke's lesser estates but nevertheless it is impressive, yet comfortable at the same time.

A maidservant enters and sets a tray of refreshments on the table. A few moments later, a door opens and Humphrey Stafford, the Duke of Buckingham, enters with a trio of large dogs at heel. The dogs poke their great noses into my skirts, snuffle at our feet. "Get back, go and lie down!" the duke yells as he comes forward and takes my brother-in-law's hand.

"Jasper." He slaps him on the back in welcome before turning to me. "And you must be Margaret. Yes, you have a look of your mother."

I look nothing like my mother, who is round faced and bonny, but I smile politely and try to accept it as a compliment. He does not meet my eye but turns back to

Jasper, swipes a wine cup from the table and gestures to the servant to serve us. I keep the thick red burgundy wine in my mouth for as long as I can, savouring the taste before I release it to forge a rich and warming path to my empty belly.

While Buckingham shows Jasper the fine new panelling he has recently had installed, I trail after them around the hall and try not to resent the duke's off-hand manner. By rights, as his prospective daughter-in-law, he should be escorting me, making me as comfortable as possible in his home. I curse my young years that encourage men to constantly overlook my status. With a stifled sigh, I realise he is unimpressed with women, especially those of my age, and hope with all my heart his son is not the same. I really need a man who is easily managed, or at least one who will prove to be a partner rather than my master; one who will allow me to have some input into the way my life will be led.

I turn suddenly at the sound of a gentle cough at my side, and to my astonishment I find the groom who helped me dismount earlier. Bewildered by his presence, I look him up and down. He has taken off his hat, revealing sparse hair and a red, flaky scalp. He is a plain man, probably in his thirties, but his eyes are kind and they crinkle at the edges when he smiles. It seems he smiles often. He points to a jewel-rich tapestry on the wall.

"This one arrived just last month from Flanders."

His voice is quiet and cultured as he addresses me in the most extraordinary way. I look down my nose, or at least I try to, but I am not equal to his height. I make do with a cold dismissal.

"Indeed," I sniff. "Very nice."

Ill at ease, I let my gaze run around the hall. It is truly a magnificent tapestry, as are the others that hang here, warming the interior and cutting out draughts. I resent being conducted round the duke's home by a servant. I hurry in Jasper's wake, my face burning with indignation. Noticing my presence, the duke turns and catches sight of his groom. To my astonishment, he waves him forward to join us.

"Damn, I quite forgot. Do forgive me. This is my son, Harry; you two make your acquaintance while Pembroke and I talk business. Show her round the garden or something, Hal, I am told she likes flowers – that's what you said, wasn't it, Jasper?"

Humiliation floods me, my confusion increased by the obvious amusement on Jasper's face. His eyes twinkle with glee but he conceals his laughter in his wine cup as the groom, whom I now must call Harry Stafford, bows to me again and I allow him to take my hand.

"I – I didn't realise who you were, I am so sorry."

He smiles, an encouragingly uncertain, sheepish grin that is somehow comforting. I find myself relieved he has not taken our chilly meeting amiss. Clearly, he sees the funny side and the heat in my cheeks cools as he ushers me toward the door.

"Father says we are to examine the gardens, so I suppose that is what we must do." He holds out his arm and shyly I slip my hand into his elbow. Together, we leave the darkness of the hall and step into the sunshine.

"Thankfully it is a lovely day," he says as he looks anxiously at the clear sky. "When I saw yesterday's weather, I thought of you on the road. I hope it wasn't too unpleasant."

"Oh no, not too bad," I lie.

We walk in silence for a while, our footsteps in unison, until we enter the gate to the walled garden. Since it is early spring, the flowerbeds mostly consist of tilled soil with a few burgeoning bulbs and some sparse blossom on the trees dotted about the mead.

"There is not much to see just now, but in full summer it is very pretty. Father said you have an interest in plants, and that you are skilled in herbs and healing."

"Well, I do my best. A household is ever in need of doctoring. At Caldicot and Lamphey ..." a sudden memory of those days with Edmund unexpectedly steals my breath "... the gardens were very pretty," I end lamely.

We walk on, gravel crunching beneath our shoes. My fingers on his sleeve reveal the cloth is actually rather fine and his tunic very well cut. I had been misled by its simplicity, the sombre hue, and the fact that he wears no sword.

"Margaret ... may I call you Margaret?"

"Of course you may. It is my name." I do not look at him. He has suddenly become rather too intense, too serious, his face too close to mine. I am uncomfortable beneath such scrutiny, and with a plunging heart, wish I were here with my tall, handsome Edmund, not this plain, anxious man almost twenty years my senior. He grimaces, runs a finger around his collar, and I notice he suffers some skin complaint; his throat is reddened and appears as if it might be itchy. I have just the salve for it in my remedy box.

"Margaret, you know they, Father and Jasper, I mean, think we should wed. How does that suit you, being so recently widowed?"

My throat closes and I cannot stop my eyes from filling with tears. I want to tell him it is the last thing I wish for; that I want to devote my life to Edmund's memory, to bringing up my son, to remembering all I have lost. But I look up at the sky and try to smile.

"Oh, Jasper assures me it is for the best, and the wedding is not to be for some while yet, until I am out of mourning. I will be recovered by then, I am sure."

"I hope so."

He takes my arm again and we move off along the path together. "I had feared that, being a Dowager Countess, you would be very grand."

I laugh gently. "It is not easy to be grand when one is constantly instructed on how one should behave, but I warn you, I have every intention of becoming very grand one day."

"Ha ha, Margaret, that pleases me very much. Perhaps your grandeur will be enough for both of us, for I fear I am very bad at it."

We stop and regard each other shyly. Can I come to love this strange unassuming man? He is as different to Edmund as an eagle from a dove. We both look down at my small thin fingers lying in his sore, red palm.

"I am an undemanding man. As my wife, you will be treated gently, Margaret, and I will endeavour to do all I can to make you happy."

Encouraged by his words, I feel my body relax a little as if I have been holding my breath.

"You, you ... did they make you aware I can bear you no children?"

He smiles a slow smile, nods his head sadly.

"Physicians are often mistaken ..."

"Not this time, I am sure. I – it was quite ... I was too young, far too young."

I lower my head and after a moment, he covers my hand with his.

"It is of no matter to me, Margaret. What will be, will be."

I look up again, unsure that he fully understands.

"I do already have a son; he is named Henry, like you. He is a babe yet, but ... oh he will be a fine boy, and when he grows up he will be a warrior, like his father."

"I am sure he will be. I look forward to getting to know him. Look, the celandine is beginning to open on this sunny bank."

Harry Stafford distracts me with flowers and an early bee that is nosing in a nearby primrose. By the time the sun begins to set in the west and we are called in to dine at the table in his father's great hall, he has put my fears to rest.

I feel better now. The future is not so impossibly bleak. Harry does not mind my barren state. He promises to welcome my son into his home, and promises his goal will be my contentment. Harry will not constrain me, he wants me to be happy. Suddenly, as Jasper and Buckingham raise their glasses and drink to our future happiness, the world somehow feels a little kinder.

Margaret's story continues in The Beaufort Woman and The King's Mother

If you have enjoyed *The Beaufort Bride* please leave a short review on Amazon.

Author's Note

Margaret Beaufort became one of the most powerful women in Medieval England. During this time, as mother to King Henry VII, she was deferred to on many matters pertaining to his rule and treated with the utmost deference. But it wasn't always so; the wealth, status and bearing of her latter years is a direct contrast to the uncertainties of her childhood.

Margaret, heiress to the Beaufort fortune, is believed to have been born and raised at Bletsoe castle. Her first marriage to John de la Pole took place when Margaret was six and John eight, the union an attempt by the disgraced Duke of Suffolk to use Margaret's close proximity to the throne to bolster his rapidly declining position as the most powerful man in England. When Suffolk, his political career in ruins, was seized and beheaded, Margaret's marriage to John was annulled. Those are the bare bones of her history and we do not know for certain whether Margaret and John ever knew each other. In *The Beaufort Bride* I have embellished the known facts and used her first marriage to shape her character. With Margaret back on the marriage market, her mother sought another suitably beneficial match. Very little is known about Margaret Beauchamp, her depiction in this novel is for dramatic purposes. She was successful in securing beneficial marriages for all her children, but that was the medieval way. In reality, she may have been a very caring mother. Needless to say, she married the twelve-year-old Margaret to a powerful, rich man who was twice her daughter's age. Margaret's marriage to

Edmund Tudor is more documented than her first, but we still have only bare facts; we know nothing of her thoughts or feelings, we can only guess at those.

Edmund Tudor was half-brother to Henry VI, a favourite of the king and endowed with lands and titles to befit his station. As Earl of Richmond he was a good match for Margaret, and the difference in their ages not particularly remarkable for the era in which they lived. What was remarkable was the immediate consummation of the marriage. Most child brides were given time to mature before being taken into their husbands' beds, and history has condemned Edmund Tudor for ensuring possession of Margaret's lands and estates by getting her with child while she was just twelve years old.

Margaret and Edmund made their home at Caldicot Castle and Lamphey Bishop's Palace in South Wales where Edmund fulfilled his duty as peacekeeper for the king. After a skirmish and siege, Tudor died in Carmarthen Castle before Margaret had time to give birth. Vulnerable and alone, she turned for protection to Edmund's brother, Jasper, at his fortress at Pembroke Castle where she gave birth to a son, whom she named Henry Tudor. Underdeveloped and possibly ill attended Margaret's body was so damaged by the birth that she was never able to conceive again.

Margaret's third marriage to Henry Stafford, a younger son of the Duke of Buckingham, provided a stable and beneficial match. The marriage seems to have been a happy one, the couple spending much of their time together, with Stafford going some way toward filling the empty shoes of Henry's father. Although Henry was left in the care of his uncle Jasper at Pembroke, Margaret and Stafford sent gifts and letters and paid regular visits. However, as the battle for the throne warmed up and York defeated Lancaster, Edward IV took the throne, precipitating a change in circumstances for both Margaret and her son.

Henry was a lucrative opportunity and he was given into the custody of William Herbert to be raised at Raglan Castle in Wales. Contrary to depictions elsewhere in historical fiction, it was quite normal for sons to be raised in the household of a knight. Under any other circumstances, Margaret would have been delighted at his appointment to the household of William Herbert, who was one of Edward IV's most trusted friends. Of course, in the circumstances after the death of Edward of Lancaster, when Henry became the Lancastrian heir, Margaret must have had concerns. Still, we can only speculate.

Henry was treated well; clothed and educated as befitted his status as Earl of Richmond. Although his estates were given to the king's brother, George, Duke of Clarence, Henry continued to be addressed as 'Richmond'. This suggests that the king perhaps intended to reinstate Henry in the future. Herbert's desire for a marriage between Henry and his daughter, Maud, reinforces this belief. Yet Henry lived in tumultuous times and was destined for an unstable childhood.

After Warwick's defection and defeat at Barnet in 1471, the Yorkist king took measures to secure his hold on the throne. The deposed and mentally unstable Henry VI was reported to have suddenly died of 'melancholy,' but it is now historically accepted that he was put to death for the security of the realm. With the death of the old king and his heir, Edward of Lancaster, killed at Tewkesbury the same year, Lancastrian hopes rested entirely upon the narrow shoulders of Henry Tudor. Jasper Tudor, realising his nephew's vulnerability, arranged to have the boy shipped to safety in France, where, to Margaret's sorrow, he remained for fourteen years.

The House of York was securely in control of the realm and Henry Tudor's claim seemed feeble indeed. Edward IV soon had two male heirs to add to his bevy of daughters, and the future of the House of York seemed set. But fate once more took a sharp turn.

Edward IV, rather like his grandson, Henry VIII, enjoyed an excessive lifestyle, eating too much, drinking too much and allowing his government of the country to slip. He grew corpulent and over indulgent, and in 1483, Edward IV collapsed during a fishing trip and died shortly afterwards. Immediately news of his death was made known, trouble broke out again, this time with the dowager queen, Elizabeth Woodville, pitting her will against that of Edward IV's youngest brother, Richard of Gloucester.

Initially supporting his nephew, Gloucester began making arrangements for Edward V's coronation, but then he made a sudden U-turn. Edward's heirs were deposed, Gloucester was crowned Richard III in Edward V's stead, and England was once more plunged into instability. There has been much violent debate over the reasons behind Gloucester's actions. It could have been a lustful desire for a crown that was not his, or it could have been a genuine concern for the future of England. Previous to this, Gloucester had been a loyal subject to his brother. Indeed, in his short reign he showed promise of proving to be a just king, but he lacked support and England was once more rife with intrigue.

Margaret, now married to her fourth husband, Thomas Stanley, moved stealthily into action. There is little evidence that she was overly fond of the dowager queen but at this point Margaret began to work against King Richard by arranging with Edward IV's widow, Elizabeth Woodville, to unite in their cause. The two women agreed that, on his future ascension to the throne, Henry Tudor should take Elizabeth's daughter, the heir of York, as his wife and queen. This agreement united Lancaster with the previous adherents of York, who now opposed Gloucester.

Henry, still in exile, continued to be aided by his mother. Margaret played a very dangerous game, sending money and letters to keep Henry informed of the events at the English court. After an abortive attempt to invade, their plotting came to fruition after his victory at the Battle of Bosworth in 1485. After a delay while Henry established himself as king in his own right, his marriage to Elizabeth went ahead, uniting the Houses of York and Lancaster and putting an end to the family feud we now know as The Wars of the Roses.

It may have been the fact that Henry was her only son that prompted such devotion in Margaret, or perhaps it was her nature; she never gave up her dream of seeing her son inherit the crown of England. Her years of unfaltering devotion to her son's cause were finally rewarded and she revelled in his success.

The Beaufort Bride is *Book One* of *The Beaufort Chronicles* in which I address Margaret's early years. The records of Margaret's early life provide only a sketchy map, but I have closely examined them, read a wide variety of historical opinion and debate, and stuck to the facts as far as possible. I have taken joy in colouring in the gaps to provide a fiction of how she may have dealt with the trials that life laid before her. In this first book, we meet Margaret as a small child, a valuable tool in the politics of her day, unaware of the horrors that lie ahead.

In *Book Two: The Beaufort Woman*, that young girl matures into a formidable player in the war between Lancaster and York.

Book Three: The King's Mother tracks her path as she achieves her goal and becomes the most powerful woman in England and valued advisor to her son, the king.

Excerpt from Book Two:

The Beaufort Woman

By

Judith Arnopp

Bourne, Lincolnshire - June 1460

The ground passes swiftly beneath me. I cling to the reins, my eyes half closed, avoiding low branches as I thunder through murky brown puddles. At my side, a sudden splash of colour; a red cloak, a blur of chestnut flank, and with the wind in my ears, I turn my head and smile at Harry.

With a grin of determination, he drives his horse harder, pulling ahead of me, throwing up clods of mud that spatter my face and skirts. I laugh aloud and dig my heels in harder; my mount lifts his head and surges forward, his nose drawing level with our opponent's tail.

Harry turns in the saddle, waves an arm and shouts something, but his voice is quickly swallowed by the speed of the chase. We thunder on and before I know it, a ditch appears from nowhere and my horse and I take flight. As we soar through the air, the wood falls silent and time seems suspended. I cling to the reins, hold my breath, out of control, afraid I will fall.

With a jolt, his forefeet touch solid ground and I am forced forward onto his neck. To my relief, he pulls up sharp and stands head down, his sides heaving, his mouth foaming. I sit up and raise my hand to straighten my veil but it is gone, lost somewhere on the wild ride, leaving my hair in a tangle down my back. I have a brief vision of Mother's face were she to see me now, muddy and dishevelled in full view of our attendants.

"Margaret!" Harry wheels his horse about, slides from the saddle to grasp my bridle, and places a hand on my boot. "Are you all right? I was afraid that last ditch would see you on the ground."

I grope for composure, try to still my beating heart and cool my burning cheeks. Managing to laugh, I look down at my husband and feign a jaunty smile.

"I was determined not to fall, Harry. You need not have worried; but I appear to have mislaid my cap and veil."

The hind will be far into the thicket by now. Harry and I turn and look back into the soft green wood to see one of our squires leaping puddles as he hurries in my wake to return my cap.

"Thank you."

I take it from him and, without the aid of my women, do my best to put it on straight, arrange the veil to hide my ruined hair before we begin a leisurely ride home.

"The quarry is long gone." Harry wipes his brow and gathers his reins, ready to mount again. On this occasion, the deer escaped unscathed, but we will not go hungry for our larders are well stocked, our cellar replete with wine. It is not need that calls us from our fireside to hunt, but the longing for fresh air. I feel vital and alive. I run a gloved hand down my horse's neck and turn again to smile at Harry.

So far, he has proved a good husband. He lacks the noble looks of Edmund, but I am learning there is more to a man than a fine physique. My life with Edmund was spent waiting and worrying but, as Harry's wife, most of my days are spent with him, and hunting is not the only pleasure we share. Harry is a quiet, studious man whose interests lie in books rather than war; he prefers to be home, running his estates and caring for his tenants than careering around the country in the service of the king.

He is loyal to King Henry, of course, but he takes little part in the disputes that continue to beset the throne. The feud between the two royal houses endures; they fight, cousin against cousin, their households forced to take sides and no one allowed to remain impartial.

At the end of last year, the Duke of York fled to Ireland, and his cousin and ally, the Duke of Warwick, took refuge in France. Now, there is an uneasy peace as the country waits to see what will happen next. For a while at least, Harry and I are free to relax.

Letting our mounts cool and catch their breath, we ride with long, loose reins toward home, and soon the timbers of the house come into view. We pause at the top of the hill to allow our attendants to catch up, and the servants at the castle, noticing our approach, scurry about in preparation for our arrival. I glance at Harry, catch his eye and issue an unspoken challenge.

Without a word, we simultaneously dig in our spurs, surprising our horses into life again as we compete to see who shall be the first to reach home. At the sound of our speeding hooves a cry goes up and, just in time, they throw open the gates. As we clatter over the drawbridge and into the bailey, Harry is just ahead. He leaps from his horse and hurries to assist me from mine. We are both breathless.

"I beat you squarely, Margaret. Admit it, you are defeated. I am the better horseman."

"Perhaps I allowed you to win; had you thought of that?"

He throws back his head with a snort of derision and, as we ascend the steps, I try to take his elbow. But instead, he throws an easy arm around my shoulders and plants a kiss on my forehead.

"Of course you did, sweetheart. Of course you did."

After the brightness of the day, the hall is dark. Slowly pulling off my gloves, I blink while my eyes readjust. Harry pours a cup of wine, continuing to crow of his prowess in the saddle until a boy comes forward and hands him a message. I toss my cloak at a hovering servant.

"Bring us some more refreshment, this wine is rancid," Harry says, unrolling the parchment and carrying it to the window where the light is better. "Damn!"

I turn, surprised at his profanity.

"What is it, Harry? Not Henry; it isn't bad news of my son?"

I hurry forward, my heart suddenly sick, and reach for the letter.

"No, no," he says, his brow furrowed as he scrunches the parchment into my palm. "It isn't from Pembroke. It is from my father. Salisbury and Warwick have landed in Kent and are marching on London, and he rides to defend the capital. I am summoned to join him."

Without reading it, I let the letter drop, and pull a face.

"Must you?"

"I have to go; there is no way I can refuse."

A thousand reasons why he shouldn't leave rush through my mind; silly things like an appointment with the tailor, the regime of care we have embarked upon for his skin complaint, the sick horse in the stable that he has been tending. I open my mouth to speak but he is already turning way, bellowing for his squire.

"How long will you be gone?"

He does not heed me; my voice is lost in the hubbub. Silently cursing York and his persistent dissent, I follow in Harry's wake, waiting for my chance to speak, but he is soon lost among a crowd of retainers.

I fall back, barely able to see the top of his head in the clamour, but I can hear his voice. His scribe hovers at the back of the crowd, quill in hand, straining to hear so he may list Harry's instructions.

I am forgotten.

Reaching for a cup of wine, I slump into a chair. I realise the futility of trying to prevent him from leaving. The friction at court has become untenable, and late last summer violence broke out again with a heavy humiliating defeat for the king at Blore Heath, which was quickly followed by victory for Lancaster at Ludford two weeks later.

The conflict between the two houses is like a great seesaw; one moment the king is winning, the next he is cast down. When York's army scattered and he and Warwick fled to exile overseas, I had hoped it was all over. Since then, things have been quiet; I cannot believe it is to begin again.

As painful as it is to see Harry go, I know it is his duty to answer his father's call yet I cannot help but remember when Edmund rode away from Lamphey on that last day. Despite everything that has happened to me since, I cannot forget that.

During the two years Harry and I have been married, I have become fond of him. It is an easy relationship, much easier than the one I had with Edmund. He treats me as an equal, appreciative of my skills in the still-room, gently encouraging my studies, and tolerant of my devotion to God, which inwardly I fear he does not share.

Harry has a gentle humour, a compassion for those less fortunate, and a wry and sometimes cynical opinion of his betters. As a younger son, he has come to accept his lot in life, his ill health, and his political obscurity. We are rich but not so prominent that we are constantly at the beck and call of court, but the quiet, country life we live suits us, and he is a good stepfather to my son.

The one thorn in my shoe is my separation from little Henry, but we have made several visits to Wales and I am touched by and grateful for my husband's obvious affection for my boy. I can never give Harry a child of his own but I have bequeathed him mine, and it warms my heart to see their flourishing relationship.

Ours is a good match, a good choice. I have benefitted from his gentleness and he has benefitted from my knowledge of herbs and medicine. His sore skin is soothed now; the nightly creams and poultices I take so long to prepare have brought him ease and, with the constant itching soothed, he can now sleep at night. Without me to ensure he keeps up the regime, however, he will soon become uncomfortable again, and all my work will be undone. I want to remind him of this but I do not speak of it, for I know he would scorn my concern.

It seems our honeymoon is over, the long period of peace is ended; our days of placid domesticity may seem dull to some, but I don't want them to end. I do not complain. I stay calm and quiet as I watch his preparations for battle, and never once do I let my smile drop.

"Farewell, sweetheart." He kisses my brow. "I will be back soon."

He moves away, and before I can stop myself, I grab the sleeve of his coat. He turns, a questioning frown on his forehead, his eyes silently beseeching me not to make a fuss.

"Take this," I say, pressing a small glass phial into his palm. "Apply it each evening before you retire."

He laughs. "My squire will think less of me but, for you, Margaret, I will do as you ask."

One more kiss and he is hurrying away, calling for his horse, setting the dogs barking. With a flourish of banners and a clash of armour, the troop ride beneath the gate and a sorry peace descends with the dust.

It seems I am destined to be left behind, alone.

In the solitude, with little to distract me, my thoughts turn to my son. I know he has a comfortable home at Pembroke and is as safe as a boy can be, but I cannot shake off the nagging worry that he might be ailing. Deciding a visit is overdue, I summon Harry's steward.

"Oh, Master Bray. Your step is so soft it startled me."

"I apologise, Madam. I will endeavour to tread more heavily next time I approach."

"I want to travel to Pembroke to visit my son. Please make the arrangements for my journey."

He hesitates, clears his throat.

"I don't believe that is wise, my lady. The armies are mustering and the roads will be full of men, and besides ... my lord of Pembroke will not be at home. He will surely be fighting for the king."

I had forgotten that but it makes me no less determined to go. With just the household staff for company, Henry will be alone – vulnerable, and perhaps in need of me.

"But my son will be there. It is he I wish to see."

"I fear .... If you will pardon me, my lady, my Lord Stafford would not forgive me should I allow you to travel. Wait a few days and he is sure to escort you there on his return. There is much unrest in the countryside..." He clears his throat again, plainly embarrassed at having to deny me. I take pity on him. He is a good man.

"Very well."

I press my lips together firmly, suppressing sudden disappointed tears. They build in my chest. I want to sob, cry like an infant and demand he do as I say, but I am too well schooled to give in to a display of pique. Instead, I raise my chin and look him squarely in the eye. "I shall write to my son instead. Ask a page to fetch me pen and parchment."

"I will fetch it myself, my lady."

He leaves as quietly as he came, and while I await his return, I stare moodily into the flames. My arms ache for want of Henry. It has been almost six weeks since I saw him last; he is growing up quickly and I am afraid he holds more affection for his nursemaid than for me. A self-pitying tear pricks at the corner of my eye, but I blink it away.

I have no time for weeping.

The Beaufort Woman is available in Paperback, Kindle and Audiobook

An excerpt from A Song of Sixpence: the story of

Elizabeth of York and Perkin Warbeck

Chapter One
Boy

<u>London — Autumn 1483</u>

Ink black water slaps against the Tower wharf where deep, impenetrable darkness stinks of bleak, dank death. Strong arms constrict him and the rough blanket covering his head clings to his nose and mouth. The boy struggles, kicks, and wrenches his face free to suck in a lungful of life-saving breath. The blanket smothers him again. He fights against it, twisting his head, jerking his arms, trying to kick; but the hands that hold him tighten. His head is clamped hard against his attacker's body. He frees one hand, gropes with his fingers until he discovers chain mail, and an unshaven chin. Clenching his fingers into a fist, he lunges out with a wild, inaccurate punch.

With a muffled curse, the man throws back his head but, keeping hold of his prisoner, he hurries onward down narrow, dark steps, turning one corner then another before halting abruptly. The boy hears his assailant's breath coming short and sharp and knows he too is afraid.

The aroma of brackish water is stronger now. The boy strains to hear mumbled voices, low and rough over scuffling footsteps. The ground seems to dip and his stomach lurches as suddenly they are weightless, floating, and he senses they have boarded a river craft.

The invisible world dips and sways sickeningly as they push out from the stability of the wharf for the dangers of the river.

The only sound is the gentle splash of oars as they glide across the water, then far off the clang of a bell and the cry of a boatman. The boy squirms, opens his mouth to scream but the hand clamps down hard again. The men draw in their breath and freeze, waiting anxiously. There's a long moment, a motionless pause before the oars are taken up again and the small craft begins to move silently across the surface.

River mist billows around them; he can smell it, feels it seeping through his clothes. He shivers, but more from fear than cold.

He knows when they draw close to the bridge. He can feel the tug of the river; hear the increasing rush of the current, the dangerous turbulence beneath. *Surely they will not shoot the bridge, especially after dark?* Only a fool would risk it.

The boy wriggles, shakes his head, and tries to work his mouth free of the smothering hand. He strains to see through the blinding darkness but all is inky black. The boat gathers pace and, as the noise of the surging river becomes deafening, the man increases his hold, a hurried prayer rumbling in his chest.

The whole world is consumed in chaos, rushing water, clamouring thunder, biting cold. In the fight for survival, the boy continues to battle fruitlessly for breath, struggle for his freedom. The body that holds him hostage tenses like a board and beneath the boy's ear beats the dull thud of his assailant's heart. The blanket is suffocatingly hot, his stomach turning as the boat is taken, surging forward, spinning upward before it is hurled down again between the starlings, shooting uncontrollably beneath the bridge.

Then suddenly, the world is calmer. Somehow the boat remains upright on the water. It spins. He hears the men scrabble for the oars, regain control, and his captor relaxes, breathes normally again. Exhausted and helpless, the boy slumps, his fight defeated.

All is still now; all is quiet. The oars splash, the boat glides down river, and soon the aroma of the countryside replaces the stench of the city.

His clothes are soaked with river water; his stomach is empty, his body bruised and aching. As the man releases his hold, the boy slumps to the bottom of the boat. He lies unmoving, defeated and afraid.

He sleeps.

The world moves on.

Much later, waking with a start, the boy hears low, dark whisperings; a thick Portuguese accent is answered by another, lighter and less certain. This time when he blinks into the darkness, he notices a faint glimmer of light through the coarse weave of the blanket. He forces himself to lie still, knowing his life could depend upon not moving, but his limbs are so cramped he can resist no longer. He shifts, just a little, but it is too much. His kidnapper hauls him unceremoniously from the wet wooden planks.

The boy's legs are like string. He stumbles as they snatch off his hood and daylight rushes in, blinding bright. He blinks, screwing up his face, squinting at the swimming features before him, fighting for focus. He sees dark hair; a heavy beard; the glint of a golden earring— and recognition and relief flood through him.

"Brampton!" he exclaims, his voice squeaking, his throat parched. "What the devil are you doing? Take me back at once."

Brampton tugs at the boy's tethered arms, drawing him more gently now to the bench beside him.

"I cannot. It is unsafe."

"Why?" As his hands are untied the boy rubs at each wrist in turn, frowning at the red weals his bonds have left behind. He pushes Plantagenet-bright hair from his eyes, his chin juts forward in outrage. "If my father were here ..."

"Well, he is not."

Brampton's tone lacks respect, but the boy knows him for a brusque, uncourtly man.

"But where are you taking me? What is happening?"

"To safety. England is no longer the place for you."

The boy swallows, his shadowed eyes threatening tears. Switching his gaze from one man to the other, he moistens his lips, bites his tongue before trusting his breaking voice. "Where is my brother? Where is Edward?"

Brampton narrows his eyes and looks across the misty river. He runs a huge, rough hand across his beard, grimaces before he replies. His words, when they come, spell out the lost cause of York.

"Dead. As would you be had I left you there."

***

A Song of Sixpence is available on Kindle, paperback and audiobook.

http://author.to/juditharnoppbooks
www.judithmarnopp.com

Other books by Judith Arnopp:

The Beaufort Woman
The King's Mother
Sisters of Arden
A Song of Sixpence: The story of Elizabeth of York and Perkin Warbeck
Intractable Heart: the story of Kathryn Parr
The Kiss of the Concubine: A story of Anne Boleyn
The Winchester Goose: at the court of Henry VIII
The Song of Heledd
The Forest Dwellers
Peaceweaver

CPSIA information can be obtained
at www.ICGtesting.com
Printed in the USA
BVHW030228130619
550812BV00003B/320/P